B

m. Cuisland

)6

37

# The Man in the Bottle

# THE MAN IN THE BOTTLE

## Bill Knox

Constable • London

First published in Great Britain 1963
This edition published in Great Britain 2003
by Constable, an imprint of Constable & Robinson Ltd
3 The Lanchesters, 162 Fulham Palace Road
London W6 9ER
www.constablerobinson.com

ISBN 1–84119–777–7

Printed and bound in Great Britain

A CIP catalogue record for this book
is available from the British Library

# Chapter One

It showed as a momentary upward flicker of an inked stylus line on a slow-moving band of pastel-green paper. At the same instant, the steady note fed to an electronic recording bank through a pre-amplifier unit changed to a mouse-like squeak which was both warning and tape-absorbed research data.

The two-man duty crew at the central control console jerked from boredom to full alert. The operator in the left-hand chair reached for the red telephone by his side, the forefinger of his free hand rested lightly on the red 'panic' button mounted far separate from the panel's other controls. One touch, and that button would sound an alarm in a day-and-night manned operations room in London's Whitehall and simultaneously activate a live radio link between the listening post and similar stations in Iceland, Wyoming and West Australia.

The right-hand operator had already checked the stylus drum and the needle gauges ranged above. Now he turned to the monitor panels showing readings from the station's robot outposts – and just as suddenly, he relaxed.

'Another ruddy poacher, Charlie.'

The left-hand operator let out a long, slow breath and felt the tension go with it. He released his grip on the telephone, abandoned the button, and lit a cigarette. Half-turning in his swivel chair, he could gaze out of the narrow, armoured-glass window. The blockhouse overlooked a flat, apparently empty stretch of heathered moorland and

5

then beyond lay the whole pastel sweep of the autumn-tinted Perthshire hills. The site had been chosen with scientific exactitude by the experts of the Atomic Weapons Research Establishment, and that empty moorland hid a score of deep pits, each containing a steel-sheathed seismometer, each seismometer linked by buried cables to an underground amplifying vault before its readings reached the control console.

The view was incidental and accidental, but it helped – helped a lot when your job amounted to long-distance eavesdropping on the dress rehearsals for nuclear war.

There were sheep out on the nearest of the hills, grey specks climbing lazily over the brackened slope in search of fresh grass. The left-hand operator watched them for a moment then turned to his companion, one eyebrow raised in a silent question. The other man nodded, his face a mask of sardonic humour as he finished a calculation on the piece of scrap paper before him.

'It's a dam' silly world,' declared the left-hand operator. He waited until the piece of paper was shoved towards him then lifted the black service-use telephone and dialled a number.


'That's that over – he's safely out of the parish and strictly Central Division's headache for the rest of the day!' Detective Chief Inspector Colin Thane thrust his way into his tiny office in Millside Division's C.I.D. section, gave a grunt of relief, and tossed his folded raincoat on top of the nearest filing cabinet. His hat followed, then he appealed to the thin, dry-faced figure who leaned against his desk. 'How about a cuppa, Phil? I've been trudging round these dam' shipyards till my feet feel ready to fall off.'

'Tea?' Detective Inspector Moss gave a cynical grin. 'Fancy it Russian style, with lemon?'

'Funny, helluva funny!' Colin Thane scowled, then concentrated on loosening the unfamiliar, stiffly starched white collar his wife had insisted on his wearing. 'Last time I used one of these was at a funeral. My neck feels like a slab of raw beef.'

'So the guest day's over,' mused Phil Moss, pressing the desk buzzer. 'What about the Ban the Bomb brigade?'

'There, complete with banners.' The collar gave way to brute force. 'The uniformed branch had to shovel up about twenty of them who tried a sit-down outside one of the yard gates.' Thane moved round the desk and relaxed into the worn leather of the swivel chair set behind it, his feet going up to land unerringly on the one small space not occupied by a debris of overdue paperwork. 'Outside of that it was quiet enough.'

It had been, but – he felt soured as he thought of the way his Thursday morning had been wasted. Acting as nurse-maid to any kind of visiting politician wasn't a task the Millside C.I.D. chief could enjoy. When the politician was General Igor Shashkov, Soviet Minister for Industrial Development, visiting the city of Glasgow as part of a guided tour of Scottish factories, the nursemaid role had seemed even less attractive than usual.

'A trade and goodwill visit!' Thane snorted. 'Phil, give me thief-catching any day compared with this morning's nonsense. Shake hands, we're all pals together . . . there were half a dozen Government types from London with him, Secretaries and Under-Secretaries for this, that and the next thing. Not to mention a posse from Special Branch and Home Office security, with a little firecracker of an Irishman called Donnan running their side of the show. And if that quartet of muscle-men Shashkov has with him are Russian-style civil servants I'll give up my pension!' Thane stopped as there was a knock, the door opened, and a uniformed orderly looked in. 'Sam, we could use some tea – extra sugar in mine and you're half-way to being a sergeant.'

The orderly grinned, nodded, and went out again.

'We've got one or two things on the go, Colin.' Moss

moved towards the desk and salvaged a bundle of report sheets lying within a fraction of Thane's right heel. 'You know about the overnight stuff, but the rest came in while you were showing your pal Shashkov around.'

Thane grunted and brought out his cigarettes. 'Want one?'

Detective Inspector Moss shook a reluctant head. 'Still off them . . . and I think it's working.'

'Makes a change from having the place littered with pills.' Thane chuckled. 'Though how the devil the scheme's supposed to work beats me. What does it come down to? Mind over matter?'

Phil Moss was bleakly unresponsive. He'd long since ceased to expect sympathy for his stomach ulcer. And he saw nothing particularly humorous in his latest attempt to escape the hands of surgeons who appeared bent on trimming little pieces off his insides. He'd discovered the new treatment programme in a health magazine he'd picked up during a raid on a bookshop which stocked too heavy a percentage of pornographic literature. No smoking, no drinking, a vegetarian diet backed by liberal helpings of strained arrowroot gruel, half an hour's special exercise in front of an open window last thing at night . . . maybe mind over matter wasn't too wide of the mark. He sighed and turned back to the work in hand.

'First on the list is a slashing over in Creshow Street – man attacked as he left home after breakfast to walk across to the local bookie's office. Sergeant MacLeod is handling it, but the fellow who was carved won't talk. Says it was just a "wee misunderstanding".'

'Which he'll put right in his own good time,' murmured Thane. 'What else?'

'Another complaint about Jock Howard's mobile pitch-and-toss school. It was operating on the waste ground behind Profirth's factory last night. Woman says her husband gambled away twenty quid, his week's wages.' Moss compressed half an hour's voluble protest into a clipped recitation. 'Think we should try paying Jock a visit?'

'With his organization?' Thane shook his head. 'Pinning him down when he's actually operating would amount to a military operation. I want to catch him, not end up the way we did the last time, empty-handed and looking like fools. Anything more?'

'Aye. One I've been working on–' Moss broke off as the orderly returned. The uniformed man crossed the room and thumped two heavy tea mugs on the desk, each with a slice of toast balanced precariously on its rim.

'Switchboard was making some, sir,' he reported. 'I flipped a coin with the radio room for the toast – they lost.'

'Thanks.' Thane pondered at the sight. 'Sam, you're pretty lucky at this sort of thing . . .'

'Sir?' The orderly hesitated. 'Well, I make a bit on the horses now and again, if that's what you mean. But it's research that pays off with the horses, not luck.'

'Uh-huh. Sam, I'd like to see you before you go off duty tonight.' Thane waited until the man, still puzzled, had departed. Then he gave Moss a slow wink. 'Like I said, Phil, let's leave Jock Howard out of the reckoning for the moment.' He took a long gulp from the tea mug. 'Now, you said you'd been working.'

'Somebody has to,' said his second-in-command pointedly. 'This came in with the despatches from Headquarters. Better see it for yourself.' He slid one of the sheets of paper across the desk and sipped his tea as Thane began reading.

An outsider, meeting them for the first time, would have decided that the two men formed an odd study in contrasts. Tall, dark-haired, burly but easy-moving, Colin Thane was in his early forties and still close to the peak of his physical condition, apart from a strangely growing tendency to need a larger size in shirt collars. Married, with a bungalow home on the south side of the city, most of his off-duty life revolved around his wife Mary, their two youngsters, an adolescent boxer dog named Clyde and a garden which seemed fated to never receive the attention it required.

His second-in-command differed all along the line. The cherished ulcer apart, Phil Moss was a few years older than Thane, small, wiry, with sparse, sandy hair. Almost round-shouldered, a bachelor given to baggy suits with bulging pockets and crumpled lapels, Moss had lived in one boarding house for almost ten years – during which time his landlady had abandoned all hope and interest in smartening him up.

And there were other contrasts, contrasts which made them a smooth-functioning team whose professional pairing was backed by a solid personal friendship.

Thane was a thruster, the one prepared to back a hunch then sweat out the result. Thane disliked the documentation, the cross-filing, the indexing which seemed to grow in volume and need every day – disliked it as much as he used it as part of the fine-meshed detail of investigation which landed more of their customers in jail than any of the back-street clashes as inevitable in a Glasgow division as tough and varied as Millside.

In a fight, Thane seldom bothered with his baton and had long ago lost the key to his handcuffs. Phil Moss used both when necessary, could mix it with any company, but was happiest when he could go his own dry, querulous way on some task which called for the absorption of detail, the sifting, grinding pursuit of a problem . . . like now.

'One of the unexpected blessings of the nuclear age.' Thane put down the report sheet and lit a fresh cigarette. 'Ever heard of it before?'

Moss shook his head. 'No, but it's handy.'

Handy was the word. Thane drew on the cigarette as he glanced again at the typewritten sequence. The Atomic Weapons Research Establishment's new seismology station in the Perthshire Highlands was primarily intended as one of a growing chain of NATO listening posts, each capable of giving a precise bearing on any nuclear test held anywhere in the world. Their instruments could track down even the most carefully hidden underground blast.

The 'bonus' was because the scientist designers had taken the precaution of setting up smaller, automatic units within a fairly tight radius of each main station, allowing an easy check on local, natural disturbances in the lonely, industry-free Highland area. Within its first week of operation the Perthshire post had begun logging and pinpointing various local explosions occurring at isolated places either just off the coast or on quiet upper stretches of certain rivers – salmon poachers dynamiting pools and estuary stretches for quick returns of saleable fish. Now the atom men had a working arrangement with the police, and the dynamite gangs were often being pounced on while still gathering their harvest of stunned, helpless fish.

'But yesterday afternoon the Perthshire cops find a body instead, and think it could belong down here,' mused Thane. 'In Glen Lyon, near the river – good fishing round there, Phil. Who's handling their end of it?'

Moss grinned. 'Our old pal Detective Inspector Roy. Not that he's got much to work on.'

'There never is – if you happen to be hugging a few sticks of gelignite when they explode.' Thane winced at the report's clinical exactitude. 'Appears to have been wearing brown corduroy trousers and a leather jacket . . . any luck with this dry cleaning mark they mention?'

'I think so.' Moss absent-mindedly reached into his pocket for a cigarette, remembered, and sighed. 'The real reason the job was passed on here was the ballpoint pen they talk about, one with an advertising slogan stamped on it. The pen came from the Redmond garage over in King Street, but they say they hand out hundreds of the things.'

'Nothing else on the body?'

'I phoned Roy and asked. Just some other odds and

11

ends that don't give any help. If there was a wallet or anything like that it must have been destroyed in the blast. But this cleaning mark is local all right. I traced it to Langley Laundries' branch shop – also in King Street. They allocated it to someone called G. Shaw who had a pair of corduroys cleaned. No address, the trousers were simply handed in at their counter.'

Thane lowered his feet from the desk, reading the expression on his companion's face. 'You've found him?'

'There are five G. Shaws listed in the telephone book as living in the division,' said Moss carefully. 'Number four is a George Shaw, a tobacconist. According to the girl assistant at his shop, he's currently on a fishing holiday in the Highlands. She had a postcard from him yesterday, postmarked Aberfeldy.'

'A handful of miles away from the glen,' nodded Thane. 'Got his address?'

Moss pursed his lips. 'He's married, Colin. I was going to send young Beech along – no option. He's the only one free, and I'm on the witness list for the Richmond trial. I'm due at the Sheriff Court in fifteen minutes.'

Slowly, Thane rose and began to refasten his shirt collar. 'I'll take it.' Detective Constable Beech was both young and eager. But more than that was needed when you went round to tell a woman she was probably a widow – then went on to ask her help you prove it.


George Shaw's home was in Wheatlands Avenue, a trim, quiet row of semi-detached villas on the suburban west fringe of Millside Division, a world removed from the industrial grime and tenemented slums which formed Thane's more usual operational area. It was just on noon when the C.I.D. duty car, grey, with an unobtrusive aerial, coasted along the avenue and halted outside number 42.

'I won't be long – I hope.' Thane nodded to the uniformed driver, got out, and walked up the short length of flagstoned path towards the house. He rang the doorbell, heard a dog bark, a woman's voice, and then the sound of an inner door being closed. A moment passed, and then the front door opened.

'Mrs Shaw?'

She was in her mid-thirties, small, sturdily built, dressed in an old jumper and skirt and obviously mid-way through the day's housework. The dog barked again from somewhere inside and she smiled. But the smile faded as she looked down the pathway and saw the car parked outside, the uniformed man at the wheel.

'I'm a police officer, Mrs Shaw. Can I come in?'

She swallowed and hesitated. 'Yes, but – what's happened? Is it the shop . . . something wrong there?'

He shook his head. The woman stepped back and he followed as she led him through the hallway to a small lounge where a vacuum cleaner was still plugged to a wall socket.

'If it isn't the shop . . .' There was a growing fear in her eyes. 'Has something happened to George?'

'Better sit down a moment, Mrs Shaw.'

She moistened her lips and obeyed. 'What's happened?'

'We're not completely sure, Mrs Shaw. I'm sorry, but that's how it is. Where is your husband?'

'On a fishing trip, up north. He left last Saturday.'

'Do you know where he was going?'

'Nowhere definite – but I had a letter from him yesterday saying he'd been fishing near Aberfeldy. George goes away for a ten-day holiday like this every autumn, just fishing. We – we have our own holiday together earlier.' She moistened her lips again. 'Would you mind if I had a cigarette?'

'Please . . .' Thane offered her one from his pack and gave her a light. 'You haven't heard from him since? By telephone?'

She shook her head.

13

'Mrs Shaw, was he wearing a leather jacket and corduroys?'

'Yes.' The hand holding the cigarette was quivering, but her eyes remained steady. 'Is he dead, Mr Thane?'

He nodded, finding silence the best sympathy.

'While he was fishing? I – he couldn't swim. I – I've always been frightened that –'

'It was another kind of accident, Mrs Shaw.' Thane tried to avoid telling her more. 'That's why we couldn't be sure, why it was difficult to identify him.'

'But . . .' Her mouth fell open. 'What about Peter? You mean they were both –'

'Both?' Thane's voice echoed his surprise. 'Your husband wasn't alone?'

'No.' She shook her head, bewildered in her imprisoned grief. 'George was with a friend, Peter Herrald. They were camping out in George's van. Didn't – didn't you know about Peter?'

It was Colin Thane's turn to shake his head. Another man, and a van – completely missing from the picture. He got up from the chair.

'What happened – how did he die?' Her eyes pleaded an answer.

'There was an explosion.' He fumbled for the correct words. 'It would be very sudden, Mrs Shaw. I'll have to ask you more, but that can wait for a little. Is there anyone . . .?'

She swallowed hard and nodded. 'My sister. She lives just along the avenue. It's not far . . . number 80.'

'I'll tell her to come.' He put his hand on her shoulder for a moment, then went out. He heard the woman begin to sob as he reached the end of the hallway beyond. At the sound, the unseen dog began whining, claws scratching furiously at the door which separated it from its mistress.

\*      \*      \*

14

An hour and a half later, the duty car returned Thane to Millside police station, driving through streets where the shoppers were already thinning as they sought cover from the first heavy droplets of a typical September rainstorm. The clouds grew blacker and the drops became a battering downpour as the Jaguar pulled to a halt outside the down-at-heel two-storey building which was the divisional office. He made a quick dive across the pavement into the main door, stopped to wipe some of the rain from his forehead, then strode through into the uniformed branch's public office.

The duty sergeant greeted him with a grin. At the last divisional golf outing, uniformed branch versus C.I.D., he had beaten Thane by three and two.

''Mazing how popular this place is soon as it rains, sir. Cops come popping in from all parts.'

Thane glanced round. 'Your boss among them?'

'Chief Inspector Craig?' The sergeant nodded. 'He's in his room, Mr Thane.'

He spent ten minutes talking with Craig, who ran the uniformed side of the division, then headed up to his own part of the building. The C.I.D. main office was busier than it had been earlier in the day. Five men were at their desks, writing or telephoning. Detective Sergeant MacLeod was in wooden-faced conversation with a fat, twisted-mouthed youngster whose eyes carefully avoided the cloth-wrapped bundle on the table between them.

Thane walked past, jerking his head towards the nearest of the others. 'Jim . . .'

D.C. Sinclair murmured a quick goodbye into the telephone, hung up, and followed Thane through to his office.

'What's young Donny Bruce been up to?'

'Housebreaking, sir.'

'Again?' Thane grimaced. 'And his brother?'

'We're still looking for him as usual, sir. Donny's always the slower when it comes to running.' D.C. Sinclair shifted uncomfortably. There was also the point that Vince Bruce could outrun anyone in the Millside division.

Thane let it pass. 'I want you to go to a dentist called Spicer in Glebe Street. Ask him for an exact copy of the dental record of a patient George Shaw. After that, take it to Headquarters – they'll send it on to D.I. Roy at Perth. If there's any difficulty tell Spicer an upper jaw chart would be enough.'

'Sir?'

'There's more of it left,' said Thane patiently. 'Get moving.'

Once the D.C. had gone, Thane lifted the telephone then lit a cigarette in the brief seconds before the girl at the downstairs exchange came on the line.

'Jean, get me Aberfeldy police – D.I. Roy of Perth should be there. If not, ask them to have him call me back.' He hung up and was busy spreading a large scale map of Perthshire across his desk when the office door opened and Phil Moss strolled in.

'Richmond heard the first two witnesses and changed his plea to guilty,' said Moss wryly. 'Left me with my party piece unsaid, but he got three years. What happened out at Shaw's home?'

'Seems pretty definite it's him. But he had a pal with him, and they had a van. I sent Perthshire a flash report, and I've another call in now.' The telephone shrilled and he reached for the receiver, nodding towards the extension earpiece. 'Be my guest.'

D.I. Roy's gruff voice boomed over the line a moment later and echoed in their ears. 'Mr Thane? It's been a while o' time since we had our last bit o' work together.'

'A spell,' agreed Thane, winking to his second-in-command. 'You got my message?'

'Aye, and we've double-checked most o' the glen since then,' rumbled Roy. 'But there's no' a sign o' another man or a van anywhere around. Mind, we're still lookin' – but

16

if what you say's right there's somethin' damned queer about it.'

'I've got more on them now.' Thane found his notebook and flipped it open. 'They were travelling in a plain red Morris Mini-van, registration number YGE 670 – it belonged to Shaw and there was camping gear aboard. He was 38, height five foot seven, heavy build, dark brown hair, small moustache. The neighbours say he was the quiet, go-to-church-on-Sunday type and that fishing was his only outside interest. You should have his dental chart this afternoon.'

'That'll help,' said Roy sombrely. 'And the other one?'

'Herrald? Height five eight, age about the same, medium build, fair hair but thinning on top, unmarried. Also in business on his own, runs an import-export and manufacturers' agency. His background is pretty sketchy, apart from the fact that he lives alone. But I'll have more on him later.'

'Maybe by then we'll ha' a bit more ourselves,' declared the Perthshire man. 'But it's a hell o' an area to ask a handful o' polis to cover properly. Mountains, lochs, a sprinklin' o' rivers and a devil o' a lot o' deer forest – and September is a month when nobody pays much attention to campers or anglers. You'll find 'em wanderin' all over the place. Ach, probably they were tryin' their hand at the poachin' and Herrald got into a panic when his pal was blown up – maybe he just got in that wee red van and went as far an' as fast as he could out o' the place.'

'Anything's likely.' Thane looked down at the map in front of him. 'But this place where Shaw was found doesn't seem particularly close to the river.'

'True enough. But there's an old forestry road near it, an' a fairly easy walk from there to one or two good pools.' Roy sniffed. 'Aye, maybe they were both fine and respectable in Glasgow. But when a man's awa' from, from . . . well, about the worst poacher I ever met was a surgeon up from London. He always blacked his face when he went out, an' used a nylon net as if born to the game.' He broke off, and the Millside men heard a brief, muffled conversation at the other end of the line. Then Roy's voice boomed again. 'Here's a wee bit news we've just heard. Your two started their trip north on Saturday. An' some time over the week-end somebody broke into the explosives magazine at Flenders colliery near Stirling an' went away wi' a load o' gelignite an' detonators. It was discovered on the Monday – the Stirlingshire lads thought it was some safe-blower stockin' up for the winter. But Stirling's nice an' handy on the road from Glasgow north!'

'Interesting!'

'Aye, just so,' agreed Roy. 'Well, I'm awa' back up the glen. But I'll keep in touch.'

The line went dead. Thane replaced his receiver then grimaced. 'So they're "our two" now!'

'Ever heard of a county force that didn't claim its local badhats were all refugees from the big city?' Moss eyed him thoughtfully. 'It's time we ate. I don't suppose –'

'If you're going to suggest I eat in that fruit-and-nut place you took me to last time, the answer is no – once was enough!' Thane was emphatic. 'Anyway, I'm going to Headquarters. I want to look in at Records and make sure neither of these two is on the files. I'll eat over there – the Headquarters canteen always has lamb chop on the menu on Thursdays. Meet me there in about an hour, Phil, and we'll go out to Herrald's office. I was told he has a part-time secretary who works afternoons only, and I want to see her.'

He picked up his coat and strode out. Phil Moss felt his stomach grumble, thought of the lamb chops, compared them to his arrowroot gruel, and decided there were times when even the firmest of friendships could be strained.


At three p.m. the Millside duty car collected Thane from the Headquarters building in St. Andrew's Street. He

18

climbed in beside Moss and their driver steered back into the traffic flow, turning south past the city mortuary and the High Court buildings, turning right into Clyde Street, then slowing as he joined a clogging, crawling mixture of traffic moving nose to tail along the riverside route.

'Find out anything back there?' asked Moss.

'Nothing on them in Records.' Thane leaned forward. 'What the heck's jamming up the traffic?'

Their driver supplied the answer as he inched the car still nearer the bus ahead. 'That Russian V.I.P., sir – he was lunching with the Council at the City Chambers. Then he was going on down to Ayr to see Burns' Cottage . . . dead keen on Rabbie Burns' poetry, these Russians. Central Division were to keep a route clear, and this is the backwash.'

'Huh.' Thane resigned himself to the situation. 'Anything fresh with you, Phil?'

Moss nodded. 'I made a couple of phone calls after I'd eaten. Shaw was a member of an angling club. I located the secretary and said we'd probably be round to see him. It might be useful.'

'Might. Anything might.' Thane chewed gently on his upper lip, feeling a growing annoyance at the way in which he somehow found himself refusing to accept the clear-cut conclusions which were so apparently obvious from what facts they had. Yet even the facts seemed wrong in places. The explosion had been in the afternoon. Would any poacher – even two city men who might lack experience – be fool enough to risk the chance of being caught in daylight by a patrolling water-bailiff when darkness's shield was only a few hours distant?

And where was Herrald? Hiding somewhere in a panic – or could he be wandering in those hills, concussed, perhaps injured from the same blast which had killed his friend?

It was almost a relief when the car reached St. Enoch's

Square, found a parking place, and he had no more time for wandering thought.

Peter Herrald's office was a room on the top floor of one of the squat business blocks which fronted the west side of the square. The lift, an antiquated self-operated cage, creaked them up and they stepped out on to a rabbit-warren of corridors speckled with frosted-glass doors. *Herrald Agencies* was seventh on the left, there was a light visible through the glass, and they went in.

Two men were already there, talking to an elderly, mousey-haired woman. They turned towards the door, as it creaked open, and the nearest of the men blinked in surprise.

'Didn't expect you here, sir –'

Thane recognized them then. D.c.s from the Central Division. The senior of the two was eyeing him anxiously. This was Central Division territory, but it was always wise to regard visiting chief inspectors as potential trouble.

'The surprise is mutual.' Thane's twinkle was disarming. 'Just following through a Millside inquiry. And you?'

'The lady here – Miss Douglas – made an emergency call about fifteen minutes back and reported a break-in.' The Central Division man frowned. 'She says there's some cash missing. Trouble is, the only positive thing we've found so far is a forced lock on a petty cash box.'

'And the mail.' Miss Douglas broke in with the shrill dignity of a veteran spinster who finds her word doubted. 'I told you, some of the letters had been opened.'

Thane nodded soothingly. 'I'd like to hear about it, Miss Douglas.' He glanced at the Central Division d.c.s, but they were more than willing to surrender the questioning. 'Let's start at the beginning. When did you get here?'

'A little before three o'clock.' She flushed a little. 'Usually I'm in at two-thirty. But Mr Herrald is on holiday, and I've very little to do.'

Thane looked round the little office with its two desks, chairs, a large cupboard and a smaller metal cabinet. There

20

was a calendar on the wall but no shade on the solitary electric light bulb. Miss Douglas had a typewriter, and a kettle and gas-ring sat side-by-side in one corner.

'There's only Mr Herrald and yourself?'

'That's correct,' said Miss Douglas firmly. 'It's a small business, just orders coming in from customers and Mr Herrald making sure suppliers meet delivery – that, and some contact with the docks and shipping firms. I'm here every afternoon, but I've told him one day a week would be enough for all the work there is.'

'And the break-in?' Thane prompted her on. 'These officers can't find any sign of a window forced or the door damaged –'

'But someone has been here,' snapped Miss Douglas. 'I know. First, there were the morning's letters – some had been opened, then thrown on Mr Herrald's desk as if the burglar had been looking for money. Then this cash box from my desk – it had ten pounds in it, and that's gone. When I saw that, I telephoned the police then tried Mr Herrald's desk. He locked it when he left, but it's open now, and –'

'Did he keep any cash there?' Phil Moss broke his silence.

She glared. 'Kindly don't interrupt. Mr Herrald always kept about two hundred pounds inside one of the folders in the bottom drawer – we don't have a safe, and a business like his often has to operate on a cash basis. The money's been taken.'

'It was there when he left?'

'He told me it was.' Miss Douglas drew herself upright. 'I had a key to the desk – if necessary, I'm prepared to be searched.' Then her eyes widened. 'By a policewoman, of course.'

Thane ignored the gurgle from one of the Central men. 'I don't think that's needed, Miss Douglas. Isn't there an easy explanation? He's on holiday. Couldn't he have run short of cash, come back here, used his own keys to get in and open his desk – perhaps even had a quick look at the mail while he was at it?'

'Impossible.' She gave an emphatic shake of her head. 'For one thing, he would have left a note if he'd been here. And the cash box – Mr Herrald wouldn't touch it. I've got the only key, and the money isn't his or mine. It's for a children's fund. I go round the offices in the block every Monday, collecting from the staffs. If you're suggesting he forced the cash box, then you're accusing him of theft.'

Thane didn't press the point. 'Does he own a car?'

'Yes, but he can't use it just now. It was in an accident early last week – he said the repairs wouldn't be finished until he got back from holiday.'

'And you've no way of contacting him?'

'None.' She pursed her lips impatiently. 'All he told me was he would be on a fishing trip, camping with a friend. Can't you trace him and tell him what's happened?'

'We're already trying to do that, Miss Douglas – on another matter. Have you a key to his flat?'

'Good heavens no!' The suggestion brought the mousey-haired spinster close to blushing. 'I've never met Mr Herrald outside of business hours. But I can give you the address . . .'

'We have it.' Thane turned to the Central Division two-some. 'Sorry, but all this could be caught up in another affair. Get the boffin squad to come over, will you? Tell them I want the place really gone over, no skimping. And I'll need a copy of a full statement from Miss Douglas, soon as you can. Phil . . .'

'Uh?' Detective Inspector Moss had been looking out the window.

'Come on, let's get over to this flat.'

Hands deep in his pockets, Phil Moss nodded gloomily. He was beginning to be infected by a definite premonition of further trouble, trouble which wouldn't cease until Peter Herrald had been located. On second thought, even that might be only a beginning.

He followed Thane out. Behind them, the Central d.c.s exchanged looks, then one reached for the telephone.

Peter Herrald's flat was small, self-contained, and one of half a dozen service flats situated in an old converted mansion in Highrigg, once part of Glasgow's upper crust area before rising costs and the servant shortage had sent the original occupants scurrying in search of mod. cons. and central heating in the new bungalow suburbs. A fifteen minute drive took them from the city to the mansion, the car swinging off the road and up a short length of wide, gravelled runway to the main door of the ivy-crusted Victorian-style building.

The caretaker, a little man with a scowl and bad breath, answered their hammering knocks on the door – the ancient bell was out of order.

'Herrald? Round the back – 'bove what the toffs called the stables.' He gave a leering wink. 'Polis, eh? What you wantin'?'

'The key.' Phil Moss fixed the man with a dyspeptic glare. 'When did you see him last?'

The caretaker shrugged. 'Can't remember. They come an' they go, mate. Not my job to keep track of 'em – I've enough worries. What d'you want the key for?'

'To open the –' Detective Inspector Moss made an effort. 'Just get it, will you?'

The man shuffled off and reappeared a few moments later, the key in his hand. 'My boss won't like this happen', you know. The folk here are a complainin' shower at the best.'

'Maybe he'd like it better if we kicked the door in. We don't mind, either way,' said Thane.

'Ach, polis . . .' The key was handed over, the caretaker shuffled back inside the building, and the door slammed. The two Millside detectives grinned and walked round to the rear of the mansion, past a one-time vegetable garden which had degenerated into a wasteland of weeds. Herrald's flat seemed the only one with its entrance to the

23

rear, its curtained windows glinting in the sunlight above their heads. The small entrance door was close beside the broad double doors of a lock-up garage.

They went in, and found themselves in a narrow hallway. To the right, an access door opened on to the lock-up, which was empty. Ahead, a short flight of carpeted stairs led upwards to the flat. At the top, they found a wider hallway with the apartment's rooms leading off on either side.

The first check took a matter of seconds.

'Either he's an untidy cuss, or he's had visitors,' mused Thane, looking round the living-room. Like the adjacent bedroom, it was in disorder. Not the disorder they found after a housebreaker had been on the prowl with time at a premium, but a milder, more domestic chaos. A coat lay over a chair back, a sideboard drawer hung open with a miscellany of articles jumbled within, a cupboard door gaped open.

'This must be Herrald.' Moss scooped up a framed photograph from the fireplace mantelpiece. The picture showed a plump, fair-haired, mildly good-looking man, a smile on his face as he held a silver trophy aloft. 'Wonder where he won that?'

'Here it is.' Thane walked over to the window and lifted the cup from the sill. 'Highrigg Golf Club annual match play championship, it says. Hey, he's pretty good too, Phil. Won this with a final round of 64, according to the engraving – over the Highrigg course that's dam' smooth going.' He put the cup down again. 'Better hang on to that photo – and we'll give the place a going over while we're here.'

They got down to the job. Minutes passed, and Thane was exploring the contents of a lean-stocked grocery cupboard when he heard his second-in-command give a sudden shout.

'What's up?' He went through to join Moss in the bedroom.

'This.' Phil Moss held out his handkerchief. It was, as usual, grubby. But in the middle of the linen square lay a polished metal cylinder the size of a cigarette stub.

'Watch it – these things can be temperamental.' Thane prodded the detonator with a cautious forefinger. 'Remember old Claw Jackson!' For the Millside division, it was both a standard warning and grim attempt at humour. Jackson had been a safeblower. He'd lost most of his right hand when he held a detonator for too long and the skin temperature had set it off.

'Found it lying loose among some socks at the bottom of his wardrobe.' Moss laid the detonator on the bed cover then scratched his head. 'Looks as if Herrald's an old hand at dynamite poaching – if he kept his stock in the wardrobe, this one could have rolled into a corner and been forgotten. Well, what do you think? Has he done a bunk?'

Thane lit a cigarette and drew on it. 'I don't know, Phil. But it's getting difficult to argue against the idea.'

Difficult? Between the unsolved visit to Herrald's office and the appearance of the flat a reasonable inference was that the man had crept back into the city, gathered any money he could, perhaps a change of clothing, and then had got out fast. Reasons? Even discounting the colliery magazine break-in as just a possibility when the detonator pointed to Herrald already having a stock of explosives, there were other penalties waiting the manufacturers' agent when he was located. Unlawful possession of explosives, linked to Shaw's death no matter how accidental that had been, was a charge likely to draw a heavy sentence. In addition, there was the likelihood of another couple of years being added if Herrald could be proved to have been dynamite poaching for salmon.

'Let's make sure there aren't any more of these around.' Thane's voice was bleak.

Half an hour later, all they'd discovered was a little more detail about Herrald's personal background. He seemed to dress well but quietly, smoked both pipe and cigarettes, stocked a good whisky, sent his dirty washing to a laundry. Letters and other papers they discovered in a drawer showed he was thirty-nine, Glasgow born, had been a Royal Army Service Corps captain in World War II, sometimes holidayed abroad and apparently wrote regularly to a married sister living in London. In all, it was the typical pattern of a comfortably established bachelor without worries, financial or otherwise.

But that was a detonator lying on the bed – and George Shaw was a shattered corpse, George Shaw's wife a widow.

'That looks like the lot for now.' Thane threw down the last of the papers. 'The boffin squad can give the place a going over once they're finished with his office. I'll leave you to fix it, Phil. Wait here till they come, just in case that caretaker decides to explore. Okay?'

Moss nodded. 'Where do we link up, and when?'

'Well . . .' Thane was uncertain. 'Give me that club secretary's address. I'll have a word with him for a start. I'll try to be back at the station in about an hour.' He gave a slight grin. 'Unless there's more trouble on the go, I'll head home after that and have a meal.'

'Might as well pack a bag while you're at it,' said Moss pessimistically. 'Even money says we're chasing down to London after this character before daybreak.'


Gerry Cowan, secretary of the New Fishers' Association, was a licensed bookmaker by trade but an angler by inclination. Any attempted jokes about the poor fish he hooked through either occupation had long since died of old age, though his punter clients seemed to be caught regularly, to judge from the fitted cocktail bar, deep fitted carpet and Danish teak furnishings of his private office. Downstairs, the faithful were queueing to put their bob and half-dollar bets on the last race of the day. Upstairs, he toyed with the chrome-plated American casting reel he used as a paper-weight and shook his head.

'George Shaw go dynamite poaching, Chief Inspector? Not a chance. I could tell you half a dozen boys who'd do it soon as kiss their mothers. But not our George. He's an angler is George . . . straight up. He's been on the club committee since we got together four years ago. See that fish up there' – he pointed to a massive salmon mounted in a glass case above the bar, and Thane nodded appreciatively. 'That's a thirty pounder, Chief Inspector. George gaffed it for me on the club outing last summer, after I'd had a right ding-dong with it for two hours solid. George go dynamiting?' His tones were shocked.

'What about his friend Herrald?'

The bookmaker screwed up his eyes. 'Wouldn't like to quote you odds. The bloke isn't in the club, an' I've only talked to him the odd time George brought him along to a club outing.'

'Did he know much about fishing?'

'Herrald? Pretty much of a beginner. First time I saw him fly-cast, he practically hooked his own backside. But I'll tell you why I'm so sure about George. He was fishing up north last year, and saw some blokes cymaging a river pool. Know the stuff? Like cyanide – anyway, a sugar bag full of powder, and you kill everything that swims for miles downstream. Takes the oxygen out of the water and the fish drown. Well, George whistles up the cops and gets a fifty quid reward from the river owners. Know what he did? Gifted half of it to the club funds and got himself some new tackle with the rest!'

One of the telephones at his elbow gave a soft tinkle. The angler answered it, but it was the bookmaker who replaced the phone a moment later.

'Last race coming up, Mr Thane.' He paused suggestively.

'Just one more question.' Thane rose to his feet. 'Supposing somebody did dynamite a pool and got away with it. What would he clear in hard cash?'

'Depends. A good pool, say twenty – thirty fish, average weight, selling 'em in the right place . . . a couple of hundred quid, maybe less, maybe more.'

'A profitable night!'

The New Fishers' secretary stroked the casting reel. 'I'll stick to running a book, Chief Inspector. Horses are more reliable.'

# Chapter Two

Thane was back at his desk in Millside by a little after 5 p.m. On the way he'd paid a brief call at George Shaw's tobacco shop, but the girl assistant behind the counter could tell him only one thing of any value. According to her, Shaw had originally planned the fishing trip as a solo expedition, then had later invited Herrald to join him.

At Millside, he found a message waiting from Phil Moss. The Scientific Bureau team who'd checked Herrald's office and flat reported there was no sign of a forced entry at either place. If doors had been opened, then keys had been used. On the fingerprint side, only Miss Douglas's 'dabs' and one other set had been found in the office, with Miss Douglas's the only clear prints on the rifled cash box. The second set of prints, repeated throughout Herrald's flat, were the only ones found there and probably belonged to the missing agent. Phil Moss had mopped up at both places and had moved on, planning to contact some of Herrald's friends.

Thane sat back and looked at the divisional map on the cream-distempered wall opposite. It sprouted a collection of flags and pins, thin on the outskirts, clustering close near the central area, each a job for his team. The newest of the pins was beside Profirth's factory. A slow grin slid to the corners of his mouth, he reached out, pressed the buzzer button, then waited. In about five seconds flat the door opened and the orderly peered in, his expression hopeful.

29

'Sam, I've got some work for you. Come in and shut the door.'

Constable Sam Newton obeyed with alacrity. Uniformed men attached to the C.I.D. sometimes got the odd spot of plainclothes work, and that could lead to a permanent transfer.

'Ever played pitch-and-toss, Sam?'

'Now and then.' It was a cautious understatement. Sam's home county was Lanarkshire. Out there, a pitch-and-toss school, two pennies flipped skywards from a wooden stick, bets won and lost on how they landed, was a regular recreation for off-shift miners behind every second coal bin.

Colin Thane leaned back, hands behind his head. 'I've had a word with Chief Inspector Craig. For the next few days you're off all duties. Draw ten – no, make it fifteen pounds expenses, change into your week-end rig, and see if you can join in Jock Howard's pitch-and-toss school. They change their location every night, and he covers every game with half a dozen minders. You know what that means – the punters scatter any time a cop strays within a quarter of a mile of them. I want to know where they'll be before they get there – and then have a squad waiting. Jock runs a straight game, but it's still against the law and we're getting too many moans from clients' wives.'

'I join in the betting, sir?'

'That's the general idea. Any objections?'

Constable Newton had none. Thane gave him a signed chit for the fifteen pounds expense advance and Newton trotted off to draw the money. As the door swung shut behind him the telephone rang and the Millside C.I.D. chief answered it.

'Yes?'

Detective Inspector Roy's voice rumbled over the line. 'Just a wee tip-off call, Chief Inspector. I'm back in Perth at the moment, an' just out from a session wi' the Chief

Constable, who's no' awful happy right now. Did you know they'd brought that auld devil MacMaster up from Glasgow to do a p.m. on our body?'

'First I'd heard of it.' Thane was more interested than surprised. Professor MacMaster, Glasgow University's chief forensic authority, was always happy to launch off anywhere where there was an interesting corpse. 'What did he make of it?'

'Murder!' The county man barked the word. 'Aye, that shakes you, doesn't it?'

Thane whistled his surprise, his grip tightening on the receiver. 'He's sure?'

'He howked a bullet out o' what was left o' the man's chest,' declared Roy. 'It was dam' cleverly done, I'll say that much. The blast destroyed any sign o' an entrance wound, an' a lot more besides. But auld MacMaster found one or two things he didna feel happy about. Things that made him think maybe Shaw had been a dead man when that gelignite went off. He prodded around a bit, an' found he was right.'

'The gun?'

'A nine mil. Mauser pistol, according to ballistics. Was Herrald ever in the army?'

'Last war. Service Corps.'

'Aye, just the boys to collect wee souvenirs. It's goin' to be interestin' to meet this fellow. But there's another thing you'd better know . . . the bosses up here have decided to ask Glasgow for help, what wi' the complications and us no' being like some places I'll not name where this happens every other day o' the week. They're askin' for you, seein' you're half involved already.'

'Which is my bad luck.' Thane scowled into the phone's mouthpiece.

'Aye.' Roy put a wealth of blunt, grim humour into the word. 'You're senior man, Chief Inspector. I don't mind – in fact, you're dam' welcome. See you soon!'

He hung up. Thane did the same, but slowly.

Two men had gone fishing. Two apparently ordinary, friendly individuals, neither with particular worries or cares. Now one was murdered and the other – it looked as though Peter Herrald had a stronger than ever reason for running. Yet what had happened? A quarrel because Herrald had suggested a try at dynamite poaching, maybe produced the explosives, with Shaw threatening to drag in the police?

For the moment, he pushed it from his mind. It looked like being his worry soon enough, and he was going to get at least one decent meal before that began.

On his way out, he stopped at Sergeant MacLeod's desk in the main C.I.D. office. 'I'm going home, Mac – while I can. Tell the switchboard, will you? When Phil Moss comes in, he'll have a picture of this character Herrald. Send it straight to Headquarters – we'll need it copied and probably photowired to all forces.'

'Sir?' MacLeod raised an eyebrow.

'They've just found a bullet in his pal.' He didn't stop for further explanation.

The evening rush-hour traffic was at its peak on the journey out of town, and he cursed the amount of clutch-pedal work involved as he steered his small five-year-old Austin at the tail of one of the snaking queues of vehicles. Three registered owners and a lot of past mileage had put plenty of wear on the Thane family's personal transport, and the clutch was beginning to show it.

At last he won free, left the main road, and a few minutes later drew in at the kerb outside his home. As he got out, a familiar tan-and-white bullet streaked barking towards him down the garden path. Then, tail-stump wagging, Clyde escorted him to the front door.

'On time for once!' Mary Thane said it with a twinkle as he came in. 'And relax – school homework's done.'

Tommy and Kate were in the living-room, watching the tea-time Western on television. He settled down with them while Clyde sprawled before the fireside – then Mary returned and promptly shepherded them through to the table, leaving the dog in complete possession.

'How was school, son?'

'The usual, Dad.' Tommy concentrated on his bacon and egg.

'Kate?'

'We had fire drill, but there wasn't a fire.' His daughter sighed at the educational injustice.

'Mary – anything happen here?' he asked hopefully.

'The sweep came.' She chuckled. 'He's a new one. Says you arrested him once for housebreaking or something – Jimpy something-or-other.'

'Jimpy Donaldson. Always was a ladder man –' The door bell cut him short.

'I'll go.' She went through and returned in a moment, Phil Moss at her side.

'Trouble?' Thane half-rose from his chair.

'No – though I looked in at the office and MacLeod brought me up-to-date. You told me you'd be here, remember?' Moss winked at the two children. 'How's life, youngsters?'

'We're getting nature study at school now, Uncle Phil,' contributed Kate. 'It's fun!'

'If it involves fish, don't tell your father.' Moss grinned, then shook his head as Mary Thane prepared to set an extra place. 'Not for me, Mary – I'll settle for a cup of tea and some bread and butter.'

'Still on that diet?' She, at least, was sympathetic. And, reading the signs, she whisked the children from the room back to the television set as soon as they'd finished then left the two Millside men alone in the room.

Thane pushed his chair back and lit a cigarette. 'You were right about the overnight bag, Phil. Perthshire are asking for assistance.'

'I'm ready if you need me.' Moss chewed his lip thoughtfully. 'For what it's worth, Herrald's car is definitely out of action. I've seen it at the garage where they're patching it up, and it's a mess – a bus skidded into him. And he'd definitely no money worries – his bank says he has plenty of cash to account. His secretary was right – that business of his needs little effort and has a surprising turnover.'

'Plenty of agencies are the same,' said Thane. 'Have a good list of contacts and you're made. What about friends, relatives?'

'No relatives here. His father is dead, his mother lives with his sister in London. I located a couple of people who know him fairly well, but he seems to have been a pretty quiet type.'

'Women?'

'One, a blonde, a receptionist at the Northburn Hotel. Tall, slim, cool – you know the type.' He grimaced. '"Just good friend" according to her, and she hasn't seen him for over a week. Her name's Barbara Mason. Want her watched?'

'Better fix it up.' Thane shrugged. 'Though if Herrald is running, he could be anywhere by now, and that includes being abroad. You know, Phil, I just don't understand it . . .'

'Why he did it?' Moss waved aside the forming protest. 'All right, I meant if he did it. We probably won't know the answer to either till we find him.'

They heard a car draw up outside the house. Thane got up, walked over to the window, and looked out. A police driver was already walking up the front path. He recognized both car and driver – they were from Headquarters. Chief Superintendent Ilford, head of the city's C.I.D., believed in direct collection when he wanted one of his divisional chiefs in a hurry.


'Sit down, Colin.' Buddha Ilford, a bulky, balding figure, used a second match to get his pipe going to satisfaction, nodded towards the chair opposite him, then tamped down the pipe's glow with one thick thumb.

Thane obeyed, his feet meeting the threadbare section of carpet where a generation of C.I.D. men had rubbed a worn patch while wondering what the man on the other side of the desk had in store for them. The carpet, the faded wallpaper, the heavy, oak-stained bookcase – nothing ever seemed to change in this room, where the city's violence, crookery and corruption were represented by an untidy bundle of cardboard files perched precariously on one edge of the desk.

Chief Superintendent Ilford took his time, sucking his pipe, his eyes downward in that state of apparent contemplation which had earned him his irreverent nickname.

'I've had a request from Perthshire, Colin. They want me to send you up to help find this fellow Herrald.' He sucked the pipe and beamed blandly. 'I've also had another request that I keep you right here in Glasgow, where you won't get in the way of some other people who are very interested in what's happened to Mr Herrald.'

'Who? What's going on, sir?' Thane stared at Ilford in amazement.

'Home Office security branch are worried about him, probably with good reason.' Ilford sucked his pipe, found it had died, and solemnly relit it. 'We had a – well, a discussion let's say. You're still going north, Colin, but the compromise is that you'll co-operate to the limit with the security people. They'll do the same . . . or so they say. All right?'

'Yes, but –'

'You want to know what it's all about. I've got someone here who knows more of the details than I do.' Chief Superintendent Ilford flicked the desk's intercom switch. 'Ask Colonel Donnan to come through, Peggy.'

From the next room, his secretary acknowledged. Ilford

closed the switch and gave a slight wink. 'You know the name?'

Thane did . . . which made the way things had turned all the more startling. He rose from his chair as the door opened, and in came the plump, apple-checked little Irishman he'd met only that morning, the man running security arrangements for General Shashkov's tour.

Donnan's handshake was brisk and business-like. 'Try not to look quite so surprised,' he pleaded, his soft native brogue sparkling through the words. 'And before you ask, I'm still doing the same job, chief nursemaid to our Redland visitor.'

'He's still safe and sound?'

'Tucked up safely in a double-cordoned hotel a handful of miles from Prestwick Airport, but peeved because someone took a shot at him and then got away.'

'When?' The news left Thane bewildered. 'What happened?'

'This afternoon.' The security chief helped himself to a chair and perched on the edge. 'We were lucky, in more ways than one. For a start, the shot missed – the range was too long. This fellow pops his head over a wall just as Shashkov is leaving Burns' Cottage. One shot and he was off – he had a motor cycle waiting, stolen in Ayr at noon. We found it again an hour later.'

'And are you trying to tell me you think this might have been Peter Herrald?' Thane didn't try to hide his scepticism.

'Lord, no!' It was Colonel Donnan's turn to be surprised. 'Look, there's enough confusion right now without making more. What matters is we've got the bullet fired at Shashkov. It came from a nine millimetre Mauser, and your ballistics people are rushing a comparison with the bullet from that body in Glen Lyon. We think it was very probably the same gun. For the rest' – the security man's face lost its humour – 'well, I'm going to tell you a story, the same story I told Chief Superintendent Ilford less than an hour ago. There's been nothing of this in any newspaper, and I'm waving the Official Secrets Act and Defence Regulations like bedsheets to keep it that way.'

Buddha Ilford relit his pipe for the third time. Thane read the signal, offered Colonel Donnan a cigarette, lit one himself, then sat back while the little Irishman rose from his chair and paced the room, his voice quiet but every word counting.

It had begun a week before, near the little fishing town of Arbroath, on the north-east coast. First, a rowing boat was found dragged up on the beach one morning. Next, a big diesel-powered trawler had come into port, her skipper demanding in agitated, broken English that five of his crew who'd taken the boat and gone ashore should be returned immediately.

'There's always a flock of Iron Curtain trawlers operating in deep water not far off that part of the North Sea,' explained Colonel Donnan. 'They've got a chain of bigger mother ships with freezing plant for their catches, and mostly stay outside the three-mile limit. We're ninety-nine per cent sure that one or two of these trawlers carry more radar and radio monitoring equipment than they do fishnets, but that's by the way.'

It had happened before, though not often in such numbers. The five trawlermen had taken the chance of their vessel being moored close inshore, had grabbed the rowing boat in the middle of the night, and had made their personal choice for freedom.

The local police and immigration officials talked to the trawler skipper, the trawler finally went out to sea again . . . and the police cells at Arbroath were readied waiting the five trawlermen coming out of hiding. They'd have to be held in routine custody until their expected pleas for political asylum had been formally dealt with.

'Well, they're still waiting on four of 'em,' said Colonel Donnan bitterly. 'The fifth turned up a day later and said he'd changed his mind. He had a wife and family back home, and he was worried about what would happen to them. The trawler came back in and picked him up.

'But his comrades – using the word loosely – had completely disappeared ashore. Martin Kelch, Vilkas Stender, Arkan Bretsun and Taras Serviev, all were Lithuanians. Martin Kelch was the one who had organized their flight from the trawler. Kelch spoke English and knew the Scottish north-east – in the chaos at the end of World War II he'd spent a year in a refugee camp not far inland.

'Our fifth man said Kelch had talked 'em out of asking for asylum here. He had some crazy plan about making for London, then stowing aboard a ship bound for America.' The security man shrugged. 'Well, that's been tried before, too. What really worried us happened when our fifth man heard that General Shashkov was coming visiting here. He went into a panic – said that if Kelch got wind of it we'd better look out.

'Kelch's two brothers were purged by the Reds a few years back – knocks on the door at midnight and then never seen again. Like to guess who was the area party boss at the time? General Shashkov.'

To Thane, part of the story was now all too clear. 'So you believe Kelch and his friends plan to –'

'The dictionary word is "assassinate",' interrupted Buddha Ilford mildly. 'Colonel Donnan's theory is that Shaw and Herrald, out on their angling trip, met them, found out too much, that Shaw was killed in some sort of a struggle, and that they may be holding Herrald prisoner until they've – ah – eliminated Shashkov.' He used the pipe as a pointer. 'He has one rather slender fact to back it – slender, that is, until we know about the comparison result.'

Colonel Donnan nodded. 'We've picked up the occasional trace of Kelch and his three pals, but always too late. The last was in the public bar of a hotel at Aberfeldy two nights ago. A man answering Kelch's description was seen talking to two men who appeared to be anglers.'

Buddha Ilford grunted. 'And from the police side, the last trace we had of either Herrald or Shaw was in the same bar.' He gave a heavy sniff.

Thane glanced from one man to the other, a faint twinkle in his eyes. 'Who finally meshed the two stories together, sir?'

Colonel Donnan gave a hasty cough and got in first. 'The Chief Superintendent has the credit, Thane. Then we had a discussion of the situation and he . . . we agreed that the circumstances warranted a joint investigation procedure. I want Kelch nailed before he tries again. How or why your two men were involved is fringe detail from my point of view. General Shashkov's visit has three days more to run, and I want to see him safely off the premises at the end of that time. Shashkov is a big man in the Moscow set-up. He may be nineteen different kinds of a snake by some standards, but he's over here on a diplomatic mission and qualifies for full V.I.P. protection.'

'Snakes usually have fangs of their own,' murmured Thane. 'He had some tough looking imports with him this morning. Do they know what's happening?'

'His bodyguard certainly know all about Kelch, and that he's liable to have it in for Shashkov – the fifth trawlerman must have used that information to talk his way out of a possible spell in Siberia.' Colonel Donnan flushed. 'After this afternoon's episode, I've been threatened with a top-level Moscow to London protest unless we nail all four, and the line it'll take is that we've been morally aiding and abetting them.'

The telephone at Buddha Ilford's elbow rang once, and he lifted it. He listened quietly for a moment, thanked the caller, then replaced the receiver.

'You've got two links now, Colonel,' he reported mildly. 'Ballistics say the same gun fired both of the bullets we're interested in.'

'But Shaw and Herrald . . .' The information steered Thane back again to his own, earlier harvest. 'What about the raid on the explosives magazine at Stirling? Then we've found a detonator in Herrald's flat, and somebody visited there and at his office, gathering any cash they could find.' He rubbed his chin ruefully. 'I'll admit the whole situation seemed wildly wrong even before I came here, but –'

'I'm pretty certain Kelch raided the explosives magazine,' declared the security man. 'All right, I'll be honest, I didn't know a dam' thing about these explosives until I got together with the Chief Superintendent this evening. Sometimes security can be its own worst enemy. As for why Kelch would want explosives' – he gave a faint sigh – 'I'd give a lot to know the exact answer. The possibilities have been giving me mental nightmares. And I'll tell you this – don't catalogue Kelch as a simple trawlerman with a vengeance bug. Our information is that there was a time when he was a qualified lawyer, before his family fell foul of the wrong people.'

'And lawyers don't think like normal people.' Buddha Ilford struck another match and puffed smoke. 'Not in my experience. They specialize in smokescreens. They don't say black is white – they prove it.'

Thane gave a slow nod. 'Which means Kelch could have planned to make Shaw's death look like an accident, then organized the rest to make it appear that Herrald was making a bolt because of the possible consequences – taking the money, planting the detonator where we'd find it, leaving us groping behind his own particular smoke-screen.'

It fitted, fitted the pattern of a man who could blend apparently unrelated steps into an organized purposeful campaign.

'Colin . . .?'

'Sir?' He glanced towards Ilford.

'There's a car waiting. Take Phil Moss with you. It's 73 miles to Aberfeldy if you take the Sma' Glen road once you get north. I'll expect a call in a couple of hours.' He pointed the pipe again as Thane rose. 'I'm not going to give you a lecture on how to handle this, but the fewer who know the full story the better.'

Colonel Donnan pulled an envelope from his inside pocket and passed it over. 'That's what we've got so far on Kelch and company – not much, I'm afraid. I'll have to stick with Shashkov more than ever now, but my people will give you any direct help they can. You'll find contact details in there, too.'

Shashkov and Kelch, assassination and diplomatic poker-play – Thane said goodbye and left. The security man had called George Shaw's death a 'fringe detail'. Perhaps it was, compared with the threat of another, more successful attack on the Communist leader. But as he boarded the waiting C.I.D. Jaguar and it purred from the station courtyard, through the old-fashioned stone gate pillars and on to the road beyond, Colin Thane held to another concern, one the security chief, even Buddha Ilford, had almost brushed aside. Was Peter Herrald still alive?

It was a concern far simpler to handle than the complexity of sympathizing with a killer whose revenge wish was so easy to understand, so hard to condemn.

The car picked up Phil Moss at Millside. Fifteen minutes later they'd cleared the city. Their driver glanced at the dashboard clock – just on seven p.m. His foot pressed down on the accelerator, the engine's response sent the speedometer sweeping up and round in a fast curve, and he felt happy. He reckoned on being in Aberfeldy by late dusk, and Thane was one Chief Inspector who didn't mind drivers smoking on duty.

With less than fifteen minutes to go before closing time, the public bar of the Tayman Hotel at Aberfeldy was noisy and busy. Detective Inspector Phil Moss nursed his tomato juice at a little corner table while his Perthshire counterpart

41

took a long swallow from a pint mug of draught beer then wiped his lips.

'Beer on duty, whisky for pleasure,' declared Detective Inspector Roy, a large, beefy man wearing a dirty fawn waterproof coat and a brown homburg hat, both of indeterminate age. 'You know these parts, Moss?'

Phil Moss shook his head. 'Not unless you count being here for two weeks' holiday when I was a youngster.' The drive up, though, had been pleasant despite the pace involved. The finest stretch had been across the high, lonely Sma' Glen road where each twisting corner was more likely to disclose a flurry of small game quitting the tarmac than the sight of another vehicle approaching. Then he remembered the swoop down from the moorland into the forested valley, the distant circle of snow-tipped mountain peaks, '. . . nice countryside. I like it.'

'Reasonable, reasonable.' Roy's regional pride was satisfied. 'The river's the thing, though. Where Shaw and Herrald were, on the Lyon, isn't bad. But the real fishin' starts here, on the Tay.'

Moss nodded. The talk around the bar seemed equally divided between 'the fishin'' and some scandal over the price of a bunch of Blackface sheep sold at the town market the previous week.

'There's a wee stretch o' water I sometimes try mysel',' said Roy. 'It's owned by a man I did a bit obligement for once. There's some fine fish waitin' the right rod. The Tay's got the British salmon record – a 64 pounder, man! A clean 54 inches long, and caught by a tiny slip o' a girl.' He shook his head at the injustice.

'Time's getting on,' frowned Moss. 'You're sure this man MacLennan will come?'

Roy was positive. 'Five minutes to closing time and he'll walk in that door, have two drinks and then be away again,' he declared. 'You don't know the folk around these parts, but they settle into regular ways. According to the station sergeant, Archie MacLennan's only been missin' twice in the last ten years – that was when they took him to hospital wi' a broken leg an' kept him in over the weekend.' He took another gulp at the beer. 'Well, that boss o' yours fairly shattered all my pet theories wi' the story he told when you got here. What do you make o' it, eh?'

Moss shrugged. He'd heard the story twice now, first in the car coming up, then when Thane retold it to Roy. Now Colin Thane had gone off in the car on an errand he'd described as 'just trying out a hunch', and he was here with Roy, waiting the prophesied arrival of the nearest thing to a witness they seemed to have.

'That's him now.' Roy nudged with an elbow, his eyes on the man who had just entered the bar. MacLennan was a tall, sparse figure, white-haired, hollow-cheeked, wearing an old blue serge suit and heavy boots. As he reached the counter the barman nodded and passed over a readyfilled glass. Roy rose and winked, 'I'll let him ha' that one, for lubrication, then bring him over.'

A couple of minutes passed before the Perthshire officer returned, MacLennan by his side, two fresh whiskies in his hand. The introductions over, MacLennan settled down in a vacant chair.

'You're a forestry worker, Mr MacLennan?' opened Moss politely.

'Aye, at times.' MacLennan took the offered glass and held it delicately. 'Slainch . . .' The Gaelic toast over, he drained the glass, sucked his lips, and sat silent.

'You look in here most nights?'

'Effery night,' corrected MacLennan. 'I told Mr Roy here all about that already this afternoon, and about the two fellows who were in here a couple o' nights back. What else are you after?'

'Just a few more questions about them,' said Moss easily. 'The barman says he remembers a third man being there, talking to them – but he didn't pay much attention to what was happening. Now we know who the first two were,

43

Glasgow men called Shaw and Herrald. Did you notice this other man?'

'Aye, but nobody effer asked me about him.'

Detective Inspector Roy flushed pink. 'You could have told us.'

'You asked me about two men an' I told you about two men.' MacLennan made it matter-of-fact. 'You didna mention the foreigner.'

'You're sure he was foreign?' Moss leaned forward.

'Foreign or English,' said MacLennan stubbornly. 'It can be hard to tell, the way they talk at times.'

Moss nodded, and D.I. Roy pushed the remaining glass of whisky across the table.

'What did they talk about?'

'Well' – the forestry worker's hand closed round the fresh glass, but this time he merely sipped – 'a bit about the fishin', like most. The two Glasgow fellows did most of the talking, but they seemed to know the third one. They called him Martin –'

'Martin Kelch?'

'All I heard was Martin.' Their witness glanced at the bar clock. 'Then he went out, and the other two had a last drink on their own.'

'You said you saw Herrald and Shaw drive off,' reminded Roy.

'Aye, chust as the bar closed. I saw them gettin' into a wee red Mini-van, chust the two of them.'

'And that was the last you saw of them?'

'It was.' MacLennan frowned. 'Are you interested in this other one now, the one they called Martin?'

'Particularly,' agreed Moss. Then his eyes widened. 'Why? Have you seen him since?'

'No, but I did the day before that,' said the forestry worker cautiously. 'In the evening to be exact. I was just on a wee walk up Glen Lyon, admiring the scenery along the river –'

'And with a net and gaff hook handy?' growled Roy.

'Admiring the scenery, Inspector,' repeated MacLennan doggedly. 'Then I heard a wee bit noise, and thought it might be a gamekeeper. Gamekeepers can be as – as misunderstandin' as the police at times, so I just turned off the path, thinking I'd take my walk up over the hill instead, preferring to remain anonymous, you might say. Anyway, I was up near the deer fence on the north-east plantation when I saw a bit smoke and took a look to see what it was – campers wi' their picnic fires can burn out a lot o' trees. But it was all right. Only some fellows camping in that old ruin of a shepherd's cottage up there, well clear o' the trees.'

'And Martin was there?' Roy's voice was hoarse now.

'He was, though mind you, I never bothered going close enough to have a word wi' them.'

'You preferred to remain anonymous,' said Moss dryly, conscious of Roy now struggling for control. 'Can you describe this man Martin?'

The forestry man finished his drink. 'Well, now, he'd be about ordinary height but thin, fair hair cut close . . . in his thirties, I'd say. A good tan on him as if he'd spent a fair time in the open. And when he was in here I noticed he had a big white metal ring on his left hand.' Apologetically, he started to rise. 'Now, unless there's anything more, I'll need to be away home – my wife'll have the kettle on.'

'That's all we'll need for now,' nodded Moss. He asked Roy, 'You know where this cottage is?'

'I do.' The Perthshire man rumbled the words. 'MacLennan, why the devil didn't you tell me this before?'

MacLennan blinked. 'You didn't ask me, Inspector, that was all.' He pushed back his chair, gave them a vague salute, and stalked his way out of the bar.

'Tight-mouthed, self-preserving . . .' Roy began a low-voiced Technicolor monologue as the bar door closed. 'I know – I'm as much to blame. I should have asked him. But of all the –'

Phil Moss cut him short. 'It happens that way. Look, how do we get up to this cottage?'

'Tonight?' Roy grimaced. 'Ach, maybe you're right. We've lost time enough already. We can go most of the way by car, along one of the forestry roads. There's more rut and pothole than surface, but it'll save the best part of a couple of miles walk. When do we start?'

'Now.'

They got up and went out, as the bar's closing bell began its clamour and the barman began his first appeal to the rest of his clients to 'drink up, gents . . . time now, please!'

Roy's car was a Ford Consul and he drove it himself with an angry, gear-grating resolve which kept Moss gripping hard on the instrument panel as they roared along the narrow, winding roadway. After a couple of miles, they crossed a rumbling metal bridge, and then the Perthshire officer swung the steering wheel and sent the Ford bounding up a narrow sidetrack. The car's headlamps showed the thick, orderly rows of spruce trees which pressed close on either side, its springs groaned and heaved as the tyres bounced and jarred over the rough surface.

Finally, Roy slowed the car to a gradual halt and switched off the lights. 'We'd better walk the rest – it's no' much further.'

Phil Moss swallowed hard, relaxed his grip, and nodded.

Half a mile's stumbling progress along the track brought them to the cottage, just beyond a point where the plantation timber thinned and stopped. In the pale moonlight it showed as a grey, almost roofless skeleton.

'No sign of life,' said Moss. 'Not that I expected any. They'd move on pretty quickly after what happened.'

Roy had a wide-beamed pocket torch and they went closer, using its light to thread a path over the soft moorland. The cottage's shell was empty all right – they went through the door space, found dry, cold wood ash in the hearth of the stone fireplace, fresh soot on the solid-built chimney. There were other signs of occupation, scraps of paper, cigarette stubs, a piece of old canvas which appeared to have been used to extend the shelter of the broken roof, a few emptied food tins.

'They picked a good spot,' said Roy, shining the torch around the rough stone walls. 'Hardly a soul ever comes up this way – it's too far from the river, and the forestry road was only put through as a possible fire-fighting route. Seen enough?'

'Here, yes,' said Moss slowly. 'The scientific bods can give it a going over in daylight.'

'If I'd brought the car up it would have saved us a hike.'

'That's what was on my mind.' Moss felt his ulcer give a sharp nag and winced at the familiar warning signal that he was both tired and hungry. 'But let's make a circle around before we go back.'

'Looking for what?' Then Roy understood. 'Tyre tracks – aye, the ground's soft enough.'

The torch's beam found the tread marks where they left the forestry road about thirty yards south of the cottage. From there the tyres had followed an almost straight course in towards the trees. They crossed the distance, stopping a few yards within the plantation's edge, and Roy swung the torch's beam in a slow-moving arc. At first there was only the still, shadowed mass of the plantation's trees, then Moss gave a hiss of triumph as the light was suddenly thrown back at them in the glow from a red reflector disc.

The Mini-van was there, squeezed into the narrow space between two bushy spruce trees, covered in a camouflage of broken branches and leafy scrub.

Phil Moss pushed his way through to the passenger side, opened the door, then reached back for the torch. Roy handed it over, and he played the beam round the interior of the vehicle. The rear space held a miscellany of fishing

47

gear, tumbled together as if disturbed in a hasty search. But the front compartment showed signs still easier to read. The driver's window was shattered by a neat bullet-hole, there was a dark red stain on the grey upholstery fabric.

'Well, that's the van,' murmured Roy. 'An' I half-expected another body wi' it.'

'Did you want one?' Moss's voice was acid.

'Ach, don't be daft.' The Perthshire man grinned rue-fully in the torchlight. 'But man, you've got to admit – it would ha' made things that wee bit simpler!'

# Chapter Three

Colin Thane drew his coat a little closer round his body and gave an involuntary shiver. The temperature was only partly to blame, though there was a nip of frost in the air on this mid-September night and the country road where he stood was both high and exposed. For the rest, the cold, ramshackle gloom of the scene illuminated by the police car's headlights was reason enough.

The derelict and abandoned Dunspar Refugee Centre, on the Perthshire side of the boundary between that county and Angus, had originally been built as a World War II camp for an army anti-aircraft battery. During that life its guns had fired twice in anger and on a third occasion which turned out to be an unfortunate, near-tragic mistake, not calculated to improve relations with the local R.A.F. squadrons. When the army withdrew, a fresh coat of paint, a few extra stoves for the Nissen huts and some clothes poles on an ash-surfaced drying green had prepared it for its next phase, living quarters for about fifty DPs from Europe, families and individuals still trying to adjust to the future – or to the fact that there might be a future.

Years had passed since the last of the refugees had left Dunspar Centre, most back to their homelands, others abroad, a few settling in Scotland. The Nissen huts had been bought and removed by a scrap merchant, only the concrete bases, isolated walls of brick, a few forgotten coils of barbed wire and a scattering of other flotsam, remained as dreary reminders of the place which had once been 'home' to Martin Kelch.

The scanty file handed over by Colonel Donnan didn't help very much.

There were the brief, basic descriptions of the four men. Martin Kelch, late thirties, fair hair, thin face and build, medium height, white metal ring on his left hand. Taras Serviev, a few years older, stocky build, medium height, close-cropped grey hair, small moustache. Arkan Bretsun, youngest, about 28, brown hair, dark complexion, slim build, smaller than the others. Vilkas Stender, mid-thirties, brown hair, height about five ten, medium build, finger missing from his left hand . . . four men from the sea, four men who'd managed to elude every attempt to locate them. The two main items in Donnan's file showed just how completely these attempts had come to a dead end.

The first, a detailed report from Arbroath, only repeated what Thane had been told before and added a few adornments. Once it had been discovered that Kelch had once lived in the area, his name had been found in old records of Dunspar Camp's occupants. Three ex-refugee families from the camp, now settled locally, had each been questioned but claimed they'd had no contact with the runaways.

The second report, from Donnan's main agent for the North East, was equally unhappy. Discovering Martin Kelch had been seen in Aberfeldy had been pure luck. Donnan's man had gone there on another task, a standard background screening of an Admiralty employee being transferred to a new secret project. He'd asked around about Kelch and his companions as a matter of routine, believing them long since gone from his territory. When he stumbled on the truth, it was too late. The trawlermen had vanished again.

But from Arbroath, the North Sea fishing port, to Aberfeldy, the Highland tourist centre, was more than sixty miles. Somebody must have helped them cross that distance – which was the slender reason why Thane had left Moss and Roy at Aberfeldy and had made the hour-long drive to Dunspar Camp.

He took a last look at the camp, turned on his heel, and walked back to the Jaguar. The driver wriggled into a more upright position behind the wheel and restarted the engine as Thane swung aboard.

'According to the map, there's a village called Greenbank about half a mile on. I want the local police force – he'll probably be at home in his slippers, watching telly.'

The driver grinned and slid the Jaguar into gear.

Greenbank was little more than a score of cottages clustered in a hollow which was protected from the east wind by a sturdy belt of larch trees. Its single street was deserted, but a few yards past the one and only general store and just across the road from its tiny hall-church, a blue lamp with the sign *Police* marked their destination.

The small, brick-built house was both home and office for the village constable. Thane knocked, and the man came promptly enough to the door, fastening his tunic buttons with redoubled speed the moment he saw his visitor's warrant card. Thane looked down at the village man's feet – just as he'd said, thick, comfortable carpet slippers. There were compensations in being posted to the backwoods.

'Come in, sir!' The constable was young, probably in his mid-twenties. Too young for Thane's purpose.

The 'office' room of the house was partly occupied by a clothes-horse filled with rows of partly dried children's clothing. The constable flushed scarlet and bundled it into a corner.

'I'm trying to find out about the old refugee camp along the road,' Thane told him. 'Who lived there, who they knew in the village, that sort of thing. Can you help?'

The younger man shook his head. 'Not much, sir. I only came here a couple o' years back when old Willie Murray retired from the force.' He frowned. 'I had a visit from the

51

district sergeant a few days back, and he was asking about the camp too. Wanted to know if any strangers had been seen around – but there've been no reports so far.'

'What about Murray? Does he still live in the village?'

'Two cottages down the road, sir but he's in the next room right now. He often looks in for a blether – my wife was just getting a wee cup o' tea for us when you came. I'll get him to come through . . .'

He went out and returned in a matter of seconds. Ex-Constable Murray was with him, plump, bald, wearing old, frayed police-issue trousers with a heavy roll-necked wool jersey and obviously delighted to be summoned.

'Aye, I was here when the first batch o' they refugees reached Dunspar,' he confirmed. 'They'd had a pretty rough time, most o' them, a rough time. Despair Camp, some o' the locals used to call it.'

'Remember any of the people at the camp?' asked Thane.

The ex-cop nodded. 'A few. They were here for a year or so, most of them. Folk in the village used to ask them home for a meal, that sort of thing.'

'How about one in particular, a man called Martin Kelch, a Lithuanian? He's in his late thirties, fair-haired, medium height, thin build. Wears a white metal ring.'

'Kelch?' Murray pondered. 'Well, it's going back about fifteen years, sir. He'd be in his early twenties then. Wait though – that ring! Aye, I remember him all right.' He chuckled. 'He made a good few o' those rings up at the camp and sold them in the village. Nearly landed in trouble when I found out where he'd been getting the metal – stripping bits o' plumbing fitments out o' the church hall. But the minister didn't want to prosecute.'

'Had he any friends around the village – close friends?'

The ex-policeman's eyes narrowed. 'I heard the sergeant was around asking about the camp the other day. You mean the kind o' friends a man could come back to after a long spell, is that it, sir?'

Thane nodded.

'And it's important?' The ex-policeman seemed to hesitate. 'Things change, you know, Chief Inspector. Some folk might find it awkward to be reminded of what happened a few years back.'

'And the friend could be a woman.' Thane guessed the rest of the reason. 'I don't want to drag skeletons from cupboards, Murray. But whether it's going to embarrass the lady or not, I'll have to see her.'

'That's what I thought you'd say.' Murray scratched his chin unhappily. 'All right, her name's Moira Brendon, her husband is Big Jock Brendon who runs Greynan farm – just up beside the old camp site. Back at the time we're talking about her name was Moira Paul and she ran around quite a bit with young Kelch.'

'I'll take it easy with her,' promised Thane.

'It's no' her I'm worrying about, at least not the way you think,' said Murray gloomily. 'Jock Brendon didn't come here until after the camp was closed. There were only one or two folk like mysel' who knew just how close Kelch and Moira were – putting it politely. And if Jock Brendon ever found out he'd belt that wife o' his from here to yonder and back again.'


A cat darted into the shadowed darkness as the Jaguar pulled into the farmyard a few minutes later. Greynan farm was modest in size, a big barn and a few outbuildings grouped round the side and rear of the single-storey farmhouse where lights showed at the curtained windows.

Thane ignored the front door – in the farming counties, front doors are strictly reserved for weddings, funerals and similar occasions. The cat scurried off again as he walked from the car to the kitchen door and rapped on the brass knocker.

He heard the clack of high-heeled shoes on a stone floor, a light blinked on above him, and then a woman's voice asked, 'Who's there?'

'Police, Mrs Brendon.'

The door was unlocked and opened a few inches, still held secure by a guard-chain. Moira Paul, now Brendon, looked round the edge. She was small, a red-head, a little too plump, and wore more make-up than he'd expected. From her looks, fifteen years back she must have rated as the belle of Greenbank village.

'My name's Thane – Detective Chief Inspector.' He held his warrant card into the stream of light.

'My husband's out.' She stared at him, panic in her eyes. 'If you want him, you'll need to come back.'

'I've come to see you, Mrs Brendon. I can come back if you want, but you – well, you might prefer to get this over while you're on your own. I'm looking for Martin Kelch.' He jammed his foot in the door as she tried to close it again. 'That's not being sensible. There's your husband to consider.' It was a nasty piece of arm-twisting, but it got results. The pressure eased on his foot, she slowly unchained the door.

'You'd better come in.' Her voice was flat and resigned. He followed her into the farm kitchen, a big warm room which smelled fresh and looked clean. A table was ready for supper, a pot simmered on the old-fashioned black cooking range, and two armchairs were set one on either side of a crackling log fire. She gestured him towards the nearer of the chairs, took a cigarette from an opened packet on the table and lit it in quick, nervous fashion.

'Why did you come here?'

'I told you – I'm looking for Martin Kelch.' There was a big grandfather clock in one corner of the room and he saw her eyes flicker towards it. 'How long till your husband comes home, Mrs Brendon?'

'Ten minutes, maybe less. He . . . he's at a farmers'

meeting over at Alyth.' She drew in a breath. 'Martin isn't here.'

'But he's been, hasn't he?'

She didn't answer.

'Listen to me, Mrs Brendon.' Thane's manner changed, his words rapped across the room. 'I'll spell it out for you. Tell me the truth and I can be out of here in five minutes. Your husband needn't know anything about this visit – or about what you and Kelch were to each other. As far as I'm concerned that'll be your part finished. But if you even as much as bend the truth then I'll be back, at a time which may not be so – well, let's say convenient.

'Now try again. Has Kelch been here?'

She nodded.

'When?'

'Last Thursday – two days after he got away from the trawler.'

'How many others with him?'

'Three. He . . . Martin said there had been another one, but that he'd been too scared to go on.' She sat on the arm of the chair opposite and faced him squarely. 'Jock doesn't know anything about it.'

'Tell me from the beginning.'

She took a puff at the cigarette. 'It was on the Thursday evening. Jock had gone out to an N.F.U. committee meeting. He'd hardly gone before Martin knocked at the door, just like you did.'

'You recognized him?'

She gave a faint half-smile. 'Time doesn't really alter people when you've . . . when you've known them well, Chief Inspector. He told me he'd seen me earlier in the day, when I'd come back to the farm from shopping in the village. He and the others had been hiding in the fields up near the old camp site.'

'And you helped them?'

'They aren't criminals.' She was calmer now. 'I gave them a meal, made up sandwiches, and found them one or two old bits of clothing of Jock's they could wear – I told Jock the next day that I'd given the stuff away at the door.'

'What about money – and where did they sleep?'

'All I had was a few shillings from the housekeeping. I said they could hide in the barn for the night, but Martin wanted to move on –' She stopped suddenly and a spark of defiance showed in her eyes. 'Why do you have to chase them like this? What wrong have they done, getting away from the kind of life people have where they come from?'

'Don't spoil it now,' Thane told her quietly. 'Did he say where they were going?'

She turned away from him, staring into the fire, thinking maybe of two young people who'd once shared a summer in the warm haven of those rolling, high-grassed Perth-shire fields. Then the grandfather clock in the corner gave a sudden asthmatic rumble and struck the half-hour. Ten-thirty. She bit her lip then nodded.

'He'd come to Greenbank to try to contact Lady Dunspar. Not me.'

'Who's she?' Thane made no pretence of being well briefed on county society circles.

'She founded Dunspar Camp – she used to live in Dunspar House, about a mile away from here. When the refugees were here she worked practically full-time at the camp, helping out. Once things had settled she helped most of them either get home again or start up somewhere fresh.'

'Including Martin?'

'Yes, she – Martin was the same age as her son would have been. He was killed in the Pacific. Martin was one of her favourites, and he thought she could help him. But he didn't know she'd sold Dunspar House about a year back – not till he got there and found it's being run as a children's home.'

'Where does she live now?'

56

'I looked it up in the phone book for him. She moved to a smaller place, Creave Cottage, just outside Dunkeld.'

It fitted. Dunkeld was another twenty miles inland, almost midway between the village and the Glen Lyon area. Thane got up to leave.

'That's . . . all?' She eyed him anxiously.

'If it's the truth, Mrs Brendon.'

She saw him to the door and waited there until he'd boarded the Jaguar. As the car drew out of the farmyard she was still there, framed by the glow of light from the kitchen.

Half a mile along the road a pair of headlamps grew towards the car. The other vehicle passed seconds later, a mud-spattered Land-Rover travelling towards the farm, the shadowed outline of a tall, broad-shouldered man hunched behind the steering wheel.

Thane's driver wondered at the smile which flickered over the Millside detective's face. But there was no explanation offered, and he went back to concentrating on the dark, twisting road ahead.


It was eleven-twenty p.m. when the police car reached Dunkeld, by which time another nagging concern was troubling Thane. He'd been out of touch with Phil Moss for two hours, long enough for plenty to have happened – and although the Jaguar's R.T. transmitter had one of the new change-net frequency switches reception in the Highland fringe was too often a matter of faith, a hopeful bellowing into the microphone, and charity towards the poor devil trying to understand at the other end.

A lighted telephone box ahead made up his mind. He had the driver pull in beside it and a couple of minutes later was speaking to the police station at Aberfeldy.

'Colin – am I glad you called in!' Detective Inspector Moss had practically jumped to take the telephone.

'Things happening?' Thane manoeuvred into a more comfortable position in the cramped call-box.

'Roy and I found Herrald's van and the place where our trawlermen seem to have been camping out. But that can wait. Buddha Ilford was on the line less than five minutes back, wanting to know where the devil you'd got to and why.'

'I've got what could be a nice strong lead to Kelch,' Thane told him. 'I'm on my way there now.'

'Better leave it,' advised Moss. 'Buddha left a message. You've to shove over to Lochearnhead –'

'But that's –'

'Forty-four miles, to be exact.' There was urgency in his second-in-command's voice. 'Since nine tonight there's been an all-areas "wanted for questioning" request out for Kelch and his pals. Two men who don't speak much English and who match up on description were picked up at Lochearnhead half an hour back.'

Midnight had passed by the time the travel-stained Jaguar reached the mountain-hemmed Highland village, and the first person Thane saw as he pushed his way through the door of Lochearnhead police station was Colonel Donnan.

The gloom on the security man's face was message enough.

'False alarm?'

'With good intent.' The little Irishman shrugged. 'Just one of these things – I came rocketing up here as soon as I heard, and arrived just as the apologies were beginning. They were two Belgians over here on a walking holiday. Just their bad luck they matched up in appearance with the descriptions put out for Vilkas Stender and Arkan Bretsun. Anyway, they came out of it all right, and the local cops have promised them a guided tour as compensation.' He gave a weary yawn. 'Well, a wasted trip for both of us, Thane, and time I was getting back to make sure General Shashkov's sleeping peacefully. What about you?'

'There was someone I wanted to see but . . .' It was already late and it would be later before Thane got back, too late to go knocking on an elderly widow's door then expect a friendly reception. And Thane had a feeling that Lady Elizabeth Dunspar would need careful handling. 'No, I'll head for Aberfeldy, check with Moss, and settle for an early start in the morning. One thing, though – I'd like to know Shashkov's programme for the rest of his visit.'

'That's simple enough,' said Donnan. 'Tomorrow is Friday – hell, that's today now. He drives through to Edinburgh and inspects an electronics factory . . . they've been busy all week shoving the things he shouldn't see into dark corners. Then he has lunch with the Lord Provost, visits Edinburgh Castle, the usual tourist stuff. Dinner in the evening with the Secretary of State for Scotland.'

'Which should be a merry meal.' Thane had read that Cabinet member's last pronouncement – blast was a better word – on the evils of communism. 'What's the menu? Pistols for two, coffee for one?'

'They'll sit down like the best of pals and spend all evening assuring each other of unshaken confidence in their ability to work for peace together,' was Donnan's cynical forecast. 'Be happy, you're a thief-catcher, Thane. They're more honest than some.'

'I've believed that for a long time.' Thane chuckled. 'What happens on Saturday?'

'Don't you ever read the papers? The whole programme was published in advance – which doesn't make me any happier. He's over on the east coast for most of the day, starting off with a visit to St. Andrews and a game of golf over the Old Course. The solid sportsman touch – he's scheduled to win by two and one. From there, he goes on to inspect a coal mine in Fife and he winds up the day by giving a private dinner back in Glasgow. First thing on Sunday he flies home from Prestwick – one of Aeroflot's planes, a turbo-jet TU104, is coming in to collect him.'

Donnan sighed. 'Once he's aboard I can relax and have a nice, quiet breakdown.'

'If he's aboard . . .'

'Thank you and good night, Chief Inspector!' The little Irishman gave a sour smile, shoved past him, and went out into the night. A moment later, Thane heard the sound of a car start up and then draw away.

He stayed long enough in the little police station to commiserate with the duty officers and telephone Buddha Ilford to explain the position. Chief Superintendent Ilford was at home, but obviously sitting with one hand on the receiver waiting on the instrument ringing.

'It sounded too good to be true.' His disappointment echoed over the wire as he heard Thane's report. 'Well, what's your next move?'

'Finding out more about the people who've helped them,' said Thane. 'I don't pretend it's a particularly brilliant way to tackle it, but right now there's little else we can do.'

Buddha Ilford gave a grudging rumble of agreement. 'All right, but keep in touch. G'night.'

Thane heard the receiver slam down at the other end before he could reply. Buddha was obviously anxious to get to bed. Well, there were worse ideas. He said goodbye to the station inspector and went out to his car.

Phil Moss was still up and waiting when the Jaguar reached Aberfeldy and deposited him at the Tayman Hotel. They talked, Moss confirmed that the Scientific Bureau team were making a dawn start to be with them, and then the few hours of sleep ahead seemed more welcome than ever.

A six a.m. rap on the door dragged Thane back to wakefulness. He rubbed the sleep from his eyes while the hotel porter brought in his morning tea and the news that it was 'no too bad a morning'. The tea helped, so did his first cigarette. Then he dragged himself out of bed, dressed, shaved, and went down to breakfast.

Phil Moss was already in the hotel dining-room, all alone, munching toast and sipping milky-white coffee. D.I. Roy, cautiously conserving his expense allowance, had gone off to stay with friends in the village.

'Sir?' The one tired-eyed waitress on duty offered Thane the menu, took his order, yawned, and disappeared again.

'How d'you feel, Phil?' Thane settled in his chair.

'Horrible,' complained his companion. 'I've got the room with the plumbing running through it. Nothing but ruddy rumbles, grumbles and clonks all night.' He tried to look on the brighter side. 'Wonder how Dan Laurence and his boys liked their early morning start?'

'Dan wouldn't. The language would be interesting.' Thane brightened as the waitress returned with his order – coffee, bacon and eggs – and began to eat.

Detective Superintendent Laurence, head of Glasgow C.I.D.'s Scientific Branch, was due to arrive at the cottage at about seven a.m. – a big, bulky, untidy bear of a man whose white hair seemed permanently tousled. But Laurence was a master of many strange skills, and his team could be counted on to search out and explore any traces left which might throw some kind of light on what had happened in the glen.

'What about Lady Dunspar?' Moss finished the last of his coffee and helped himself from Thane's pot.

'Try and leave a little –' The sarcasm was wasted. 'We'll wait until Dan has had a chance to look around. After that, you and I'll take a trip over to Dunkeld and see how far we can get her to talk.'

'Going to be difficult?'

'Probably. Kelch seemed pretty sure that she'd be on his side. He was always her favourite among the refugees, and if he did reach her, she's likely to try hard to cover it up.'

'If she thinks of him as just a plain, honest trawlerman who wants to get away to a new life, that's one thing.'

61

Moss frowned. 'But won't she probably change her mind when she hears what's been going on?'

'I wouldn't bet on it.' Thane shook his head.

Breakfast over, they walked the short distance from the hotel to the police station. Their car was parked outside, washed and cleaned, and Moss guided the driver on the twisting route to the cottage, finding acid amusement in the way the uniformed man at the wheel winced each time the Jaguar's wheels splashed a spattering way through the muddy pools of the forestry track.

Two vehicles were already parked at the edge of the clearing. One was a country car, the other was the big sand-coloured van which was the Scientific Bureau's mobile lab. unit. They parked in line, then the two Millside men walked over to the group of figures at work by the cottage.

'Morning.' Dan Laurence, a cigarette drooping from one corner of his mouth, stumped across to meet them. His heavy overcoat was unbuttoned, tobacco ash strewed the front of his jacket. 'About time you got here – we may need someone to run errands. Not you, though, Moss. You're too dam' fragile.'

Thane grinned. 'Any luck yet, Dan?'

'For the –' Laurence groaned at the way in which non-specialists seemed to expect instant miracles. 'I've got the lads on a general examination of the place. We've got the photographic side buttoned up, and we're finding any amount of fingerprints, mostly on old food tins. But they won't mean much until we get something or somebody to compare them against – unless you can produce a nice bundle of two-hand record cards for this bunch.'

'Can't oblige,' said Thane dryly. 'Dan, you've already got sample prints of Herrald from his flat and office –'

'Prints we think might belong to Herrald,' corrected the Bureau chief. 'I'm ahead of you, Colin. I left word for a man to go round to Shaw's home and do the same there, and Perth have done their best at the mortuary.'

'Seen the van yet?'

'On my way there now. Willie!' Laurence gave a bellow towards the cottage and a young, camera-laden detective hurried towards him. 'Right, son, we're going over to the Mini. Nip on first and get a picture o' those tyre marks before somebody's big feet squash them flat.'

The photographer hurried off, and they crossed at a more leisurely pace to where the little red vehicle still lay undisturbed. Two county men stood guard beside it, and D.I. Roy pushed his way into view from the trees beyond. The Perthshire man was tired-eyed. For him, the job was now forty hours old, with sleep a tiny fraction of that time.

'Nothing's been touched,' he assured the Bureau chief.

'That makes a change, anyway,' grunted Laurence. 'Once we're finished, I'll want the van moved to a garage, somewhere private where we can take it apart if we need to – can you fix that?'

'Easily enough.'

'Well, I won't mess around too much for the moment.' Laurence touched the blood stain on the driver's seat in experimental fashion, peered at the bullet-holed window, grunted again, and took a jeweller's glass from his pocket for a closer inspection. 'Aye, the angle's about right. Mac-Master took the bullet out of Shaw's chest, didn't he?'

'Wait a moment and you can ask him yourself.' Thane nodded towards the track, where a big, old-fashioned Rolls Royce was purring to a halt beside the other vehicles. Professor MacMaster stayed inside the limousine for a moment, then crossed towards them, the legs of his immaculately creased black trousers tucked into the tops of a pair of stout wellington boots.

'Busy, gentlemen?' He looked around and gave a sniff. 'I thought I'd come over and see what was happening – but I won't interfere, Superintendent.'

A glint of devilry appeared on Dan Laurence's face. 'Just

stay and watch as much as you want, Professor. There's no harm in a man learning.'

'I think I'll get back to the cottage,' said Thane hastily. He'd seen the university expert and Laurence become embroiled before . . . they worked best when scoring points off one another, but it was no place for an innocent bystander. 'Roy, there's a job I'd like you to tackle. You told Moss this track is more or less a fire-fighting road from this point on. Does that mean it comes to a dead end?'

The county man nodded. 'It's on that map I gave Moss last night. There's only one way a vehicle can get out o' here, an' that's back the way we came.'

'So anything coming up would have to make a turn, which would probably mean driving off the road.' Thane pressed one foot into the soft, muddy soil and examined the result. 'It might leave tyre marks – and I want this section of road checked for them.'

'What's the idea?' demanded Moss.

'Nothing spectacular, Phil. I'd just like to know if the Mini was the only vehicle to come this way and, if it was, whether it travelled the route more than once.'

Detective Inspector Roy scratched one ear. 'I think I know what you mean. I might as well take care o' it now – I've nothing else on my plate.'

'Let's split it,' suggested Moss. 'I'll take one side of the track, you take the other. Right?' He glanced for Thane's approval.

'It'll save time,' agreed Thane. He watched them set off, then continued on his own towards the cottage.

Nothing spectacular, he'd said. Checking out a possibility which might mean anything or nothing – it happened all the time, the gathering, sorting, storing, rejecting. How had Kelch reached the ruined cottage in the first instance? Had he stumbled on it, known of it from those earlier days, or been told about it? Had he and the others hitch-hiked, walked, or been taken by some outside friend who could supply a car? Maybe Lady Dunspar would supply

64

some of the answers. He stopped at the door of the old cottage and found himself scowling at the weathered stonework. The cottage knew – but Thane dealt in people, he'd have to wait on Laurence and MacMaster to tell him what, if anything, they could learn within its walls.

He went in, to find one of the Scientific Branch men busy gathering his equipment together.

'We've almost finished here, sir,' greeted the man. 'Just don't touch what's left of that window frame in the corner wall until I've had a look at it, will you?'

'I'll keep clear.' Powder spray and camel-hair brushes had been busy, light grey smudges of fingerprint powder were all around showing the work completed. Another of Laurence's men was over by a now neat and orderly line of opened tins and debris of various kinds collected from about the cottage.

The man looked up, his face wrinkled in disgust. 'They weren't short of groceries anyway, sir. And what they've left behind has gone well and truly bad – some of it even has the beginnings of mould sprouting. Makes trying to get dabs from the stuff pretty awkward.'

Thane came closer, took one sniff, and retired before the mixture of rancid odours which hit his nostrils. Over by the fireplace the situation was easier, a collection of cigarette butts laid out for laboratory tests aimed at saliva grouping. He took out a cigarette of his own, lit it, then frowned and knelt as he caught sight of a scrap of blue paper lying between the edges of two of the damp stone slabs which formed the cottage floor.

The paper slipped free, a torn fragment less than two inches in length. He felt its texture and hardly needed the fraction of printed lettering just short of the torn edge to know where it had come from. He'd seen too many similar pieces of coloured paper after too many safe-blowings to fail to recognize part of the outer wrappings from a stick of gelignite.

'Better take care of this.' He handed the paper to the

nearest of Laurence's men, who slipped it into a small plastic envelope for safe keeping. It was a mere thread of evidence pointing to explosives having been kept in the cottage. On its own it would mean nothing in court. Side by side with other facts, other threads, it could help weave a net of circumstantial truth no jury could ignore.

Thane walked back to the doorway and looked out. Now and again a bright quiver of light came from the direction of the trees, the police photographer's electronic flash at work lighting the gloom around the red Mini-van. As he watched, Professor MacMaster's gaunt figure stepped out of the trees and loped awkwardly towards him.

'Waiting and hoping, Chief Inspector?' The forensic expert gave the equivalent of a smile. 'Little assistance I can give you for the moment, I'm afraid – though I always enjoy these field study expeditions. A chance to get out into the fresh country air, good for the lungs. If the average citizen had any idea of the appearance of his lungs, the view I get of them, he'd come rushing out to a place like this, away from the soot.'

'The thought's enough for me,' said Thane dryly. 'You're finished, Professor?'

'Apart from a glimpse here.' MacMaster sucked his teeth reflectively. 'I've asked Laurence to let me have certain items for laboratory examination, of course . . . a sample of the blood staining on the van seat among them. Tell me, do you know if the missing man –'

'Herrald?'

'Is that his name? Ah well, do you know if he has any record of hospital admission? If he has, their records should contain his blood group and I may need that if the sample doesn't match against – ah – Shaw.'

'We can find out for you.'

'Good.' The forensic expert was satisfied. 'Well, I won't keep you back.' He gave a brief nod and went into the cottage. Thane took another long draw on his cigarette, then set off towards the parked line of cars at the track's edge. His driver saw him coming, broke off the conversation he'd been having with his opposite numbers from the other vehicles, and hovered warily beside the Jaguar's bonnet.

'Anything fresh, sir?'

'Only the air, according to the professor,' said Thane regretfully. 'Better stay around – I'll need the car in a minute or two.' He turned away as Phil Moss and D.I. Roy trudged into sight, returning from their search of the track's verges. One look at their faces was enough.

'Out of luck, Colin,' declared his second-in-command. 'There's a turning place about a hundred yards on, hard rock and gravel wide enough to swing a truck. If anyone did drive up here they knew about it and used it – we checked a clear quarter mile up and down from it, but there's no sign of tyre marks.'

'The forestry commission build a lot o' these turning places,' contributed Roy gloomily. 'If they didn't, their vehicles would be bogged down in the winter.'

'Instead, we're bogged down.' Thane took it fairly philosophically. 'I'd like you to stay here and keep an eye on things, Roy – oh, and Professor MacMaster has a query you'd better pass on to Glasgow as soon as you get a chance. He wants to know Herrald's blood group. If you need us in a hurry, we'll be visiting Lady Dunspar.'

Roy hesitated. 'Eh . . . don't take this the wrong way, either o' you. But, well, she's a woman that's liked around these parts. She does a lot o' good for folk, without makin' a fuss about it.'

'Which is exactly why I think she'll know more than anyone about Martin Kelch. But I'll go easy with her . . . as easy as she allows.' Thane glanced at his watch. 'We should be there by ten-thirty – and let's hope she's in a friendly mood.'

# Chapter Four

Lady Elizabeth Dunspar's home was a small, slightly old-fashioned villa with white walls, a red-tiled roof and a setting straight from a chocolate box lid. Its front faced on to a long stretch of rich, carefully mown lawn reaching down to the very bank of the River Tay, at that point a silver-smooth, fast-flowing sheet of water. Only a flood level marker pole set near the edge showed that there could be occasions when the placid Tay showed a rougher, wilder mood. To the rear of the house, a high hedge shielded the kitchen garden from the main road and a short, rhododendron-lined driveway ran from the road to a wide, gravelled parking place. All around, the mountains and forests had edged back to form a fringe to a valley of rich, cattle-filled grazing land.

Thane's car crunched to a gentle halt on the gravel and the two detectives went on together the last few yards.

'Nicely kept.' Thane ran an envious eye over the weeded, well-raked, carefully pruned beds of roses which flanked either side of the front porch.

'By a full-time gardener, I'll bet,' said Moss. 'This lot would do me when I start drawing pension.'

They heard a soft chuckle of laughter and turned. The slim, sun-tanned woman standing behind them where she'd stepped from the bushes was probably about sixty. Her iron grey hair was covered by a large flop-brimmed hat. She wore gardening gloves, slacks, and a dark green sweater.

'I'm the gardener.' She smiled again. 'Was the rest a prelude to a proposal?'

Thane grinned. 'Lady Dunspar?'

'Well, at least you didn't take me for the odd-job woman – that's the usual reaction.' The smile lingered. 'Can I help you?'

He carried out the introductions and watched the smile fade to mere politeness.

'You'd better come inside – use the doormat, please.'

They obeyed meekly and followed her through a small hallway and into the villa's lounge, L-shaped, gaily decorated, with wide french windows looking straight out on to the lawn and the river beyond.

'Sit down, please.' She gestured them towards two of the several heavy-framed armchairs which were placed round a copy Adam fireplace in pink marble. The polished wood floor had most of its area covered by a tassel-fringed Persian carpet in lime green, and a big radio-stereogram unit, framed in maple, occupied a length of wall to one side.

Phil Moss gave the room a casual, appreciative inspection then glanced at the two portraits hung on the wall behind the stereo unit. One showed a dark-haired youngster in R.A.F. uniform, pilot's wings on the tunic, the other was an equally dark-haired schoolgirl who, despite her chubbiness and broad, teenage grin, seemed vaguely familiar. He'd seen her somewhere, decided Moss – probably in newspaper photographs or within the covers of one of the glossy magazines he sampled in the waiting room at his doctor's surgery.

Yet . . . he postponed the puzzle as Lady Dunspar sat down opposite them.

'Well, Chief Inspector?' Firm and assured, she turned towards Thane.

'I think you know why we're here, Lady Dunspar –'

'Do I?' She blinked deliberately and this time the smile was even colder. 'Perhaps you'd better tell me.'

69

'In that case . . .' Thane switched his approach. 'Would it save time if I said we know Martin Kelch and three companions tried to locate you at Greenbank? That they were told you now lived near Dunkeld and left Greenbank to come here?'

She was silent for a moment, then gave a slight shrug. 'I don't need to ask where you got that information – and I can guess one way in which you'd obtain it. An unpleasant way. Well, I'm not a young woman who kept a secret from her husband, Chief Inspector. I'm a widow, reasonably independent, and I've never given a twopenny damn for authority. If I have to make a decision I let my own mind and heart tell me what to do.'

'Did they tell you to help Martin Kelch?'

She drew herself a little more upright in the chair. 'Have I said he was here?'

'You've more or less admitted it, Lady Dunspar. It would be a natural enough reaction to help him, just the way you did before when he was a young refugee. You always had – well, a soft spot for him, didn't you?' He watched her closely.

'That's true.' Her face softened. 'He was the same age as – as my son would have been. Martin had the same kind of nature too – affectionate, a little reckless, sure of his own ability. He was all on his own in that camp, and when word finally did come that his family had been located and that he could go back to Lithuania I asked him not to do it. I wanted him to stay with me – be more or less an adopted son. He refused, Chief Inspector. He told me his place was back with them. Once he'd gone I had one or two letters then silence, no word –'

'Until he arrived at this house a few nights ago?'

'Yes, he was here.' Lady Dunspar glimpsed the notebook appearing in Phil Moss's hand and shook her head. 'Put that away, please. I'm prepared to talk about this in a civilized fashion, but I point-blank refuse to make anything approaching a statement.'

Thane gave a faint nod and his second-in-command tucked the notebook back in his pocket.

'Martin arrived here on the Friday afternoon . . . his friends hid in one of the fields outside until he signalled them it was safe. I live alone, Chief Inspector, except for a housekeeper who lives out and has Saturday and Sunday off, so as soon as she had gone they were quite safe.'

'And they stayed in this house?'

'Yes.'

'For how long?'

She shook her head. 'I've said enough – except that Martin and his friends came here in need of help and I did all I could to give them that help.'

'Help for what purpose, Lady Dunspar?' A new, harder note underlined his question. 'To get to America – or did they know then about General Shashkov's visit, and have a different purpose?'

Lady Dunspar rose to her feet. 'I don't know what that's supposed to mean. But unless you intend to bring some charge against me, I suggest you leave.'

He shook his head. 'Not yet. I didn't come north just to round up a bunch of trawlermen who've jumped from a ship, Lady Dunspar. I'm trying to find four men who now have a small arsenal of gelignite in their possession, four men who've already had one try at killing a visiting diplomat. All right, maybe you don't care about Shashkov, or what the consequences could be. Maybe you feel that men like Kelch are justified if they see killing the man as a mixture of retribution and justice, and to hell with the consequences. . . .'

'Martin would have nothing to do with –'

'Wouldn't he?' Thane walked over and stood directly in front of her. 'There's more, Lady Dunspar. I'm thinking of two anglers who came north for a holiday. On Wednesday one of these men was shot dead. His friend is missing. We found their van a short distance from an old cottage where we know Kelch and the others had been hiding. Let's forget Shashkov, Lady Dunspar. But what about an ordinary little man called George Shaw? And what about his wife? I was the one who had to tell her that he'd been killed, that he wouldn't be back from that fishing trip.' He took a deep breath and let his hands fall by his sides. 'Or do they make no difference, Lady Dunspar?'

Suddenly, she seemed to have aged. She spoke in a near daze, making no attempt to hide the tremor in her voice. 'This cottage – where was it?'

'Near Glen Lyon, beside a forestry road. You know it?'

She bit her lip, and when she spoke it wasn't to answer. 'But – but it happened on Wednesday, you said! Martin couldn't have been responsible, in any way. On Wednesday he was –' She stopped short and bit her lip again.

'He was what, Lady Dunspar?'

'I'm sorry . . .' It came out as a near whisper. 'All I'm prepared to say at this moment is that neither Martin nor his friends are in this house and that I personally no longer know their whereabouts. You're at liberty to search my home if you don't believe me . . . that's all, Chief Inspector. I – I would like a little time to consider what you've told me.'

Thane looked at her for a long moment then nodded. 'I'll take your word they aren't here. But time's a precious factor as far as we're concerned, Lady Dunspar – don't waste too much of it making up your mind what to do. Other lives could depend on it.'

'This afternoon – early?'

'All right.' He nodded across to Moss, who rose from his chair. 'I've taken your word on one point. Will you give it on another – that you won't try to contact them by telephone or any other way?'

'I won't.' She straightened her shoulders a little. 'I – I'll see you to the door.'

Still curious, Phil Moss began to follow them then stopped beside the portrait of the girl. There was something nudging his mind about that face, the same and yet different from another he'd known. He gave a mild courtesy cough.

'Lady Dunspar, this girl – is she your daughter?'

A surprise flicker of what could have been either panic or anger crossed her face. 'Yes. Why?'

'I just wondered.'

She led them the rest of the way to the house door, said goodbye, and closed it quickly behind them.

'What the heck made you ask about that painting?' demanded Thane as they crunched their way back across the gravel to the car. 'Since when were you interested in family portraits?'

'I don't really know,' admitted his companion. 'Just a feeling I've seen that face somewhere, and recently. Yet it was different somehow – ach, I give up.'

'Her son was killed over fifteen years ago,' reminded Thane. 'The girl's portrait was probably painted at the same time as her brother's – your schoolgirl will be a woman by now.'

They reached the car and climbed aboard. As the Jaguar's door closed again, the driver gave an inquiring glance.

'It's your turn to play detective,' Thane told him. 'I want to locate the local telephone exchange – the phone in that house was non-automatic, so we shouldn't have far to go.'

'Thinking of arranging a phone tap?' asked Moss as the car pulled away. 'That can mean trouble – and if she knows where they are she could be calling them right now.'

'She gave her word, Phil.' Thane took out his cigarettes, lit one, and leaned back as the car started off. 'With that kind of woman, her word is her bond. And I'm pretty certain that what she told us was the absolute truth – as far as it goes. No, I want to have a look through the exchange's list of trunk calls passed from her number. There may be a lead there, a lead to the type of help she gave to Kelch – and before we go back to see her, I'd like to have some idea of what she's able to tell us.'

The telephone exchange, when they found it, was located in a small back room behind a shop which combined the role of post office, newsagent and grocery store for a tiny clachan of houses about two miles distant. The shopkeeper's wife, who also acted as switchboard girl, took care of a customer's order for two tins of diced fruit and a bottle of washing-up detergent then lifted the counter flap and ushered the two C.I.D. men through to the rear.

'Lady Dunspar's telephone?' She showed instant amazement. 'Is something wrong up at the house?'

'Nothing to concern yourself about,' Thane reassured her. 'Have you got the list of numbers?'

'Aye, it's in this book.' She lifted a black ledger from beside a stacked tray of bread then paused unhappily. 'You won't mind if I make a wee call to the district supervisor at Dunkeld exchange, just to make sure it's all right to show you it?'

Thane told her to go ahead. They heard only her side of the brief conversation, but when she'd finished and unplugged the line on the board she was satisfied.

'Help yourselves,' she invited.

Thane reached for the ledger then stopped as the driver from their car came through the counter-flap and into the room.

'Something up?'

'Looks that way, Chief Inspector,' said the driver. 'The car radio's still crackling like the devil was inside it, but the message was you've to call Edinburgh city headquarters – they've a priority call for you.'

'Thanks.' He turned to the shopkeeper's wife as the man went back towards the car. 'Can you get me through?' She set to work, and he frowned, then handed the ledger to Moss. 'Phil, find any numbers called from that house since last Friday. Once I've spoken to Edinburgh we can contact

Post Office Information and match addresses against her calls.'

Moss pushed his way further back into the shop, found a seat on a sack of potatoes, and began flicking the trunk lists. At the board, the shopkeeper's wife looked up. 'I've got them on the line now, sir.' She made a fast crocheting movement with one of the plugs, then pointed to an extension receiver mounted on the wall. 'Will you take it there?'

He nodded, then touched her on the arm. 'Mind going outside?'

'But the switchboard –'

'I won't be long.'

She wasn't pleased, but she went. As the door closed behind her, he lifted the receiver. 'Thane –'

'Where the hell have you been hiding?' Colonel Donnan's voice came faint and despairingly over the line. 'It's taken me dam' near fifteen minutes to get hold of you – where are you anyway?'

'In a midget-sized telephone exchange near Dunkeld. Why?' Thane refused to be ruffled, but the temptation was there.

'You'd probably be a dam' sight nearer to Kelch if you were here in Edinburgh.' The security chief's Irish brogue thickened and betrayed his tension. 'It's just forty minutes since somebody had a good try at blowing General Shashkov sky-high – a bomb in a pillar-box just opposite the electronics factory he was visiting. The box went up with a bang exactly as Shashkov's car passed it!'

'What's the casualty list?' Thane rapped the query while Moss crowded closer, straining his ears to catch the distant end of the conversation.

'Five,' snarled Donnan. 'The car was damaged, the driver cut by flying glass, but Shashkov came out of it without a mark. One motor cycle cop is in hospital with a fractured skull – he was between the car and the bomb, and he's on the danger list. One of my boys and two beat cops are in the same hospital having chunks of pillar-box picked out of them. It was cast iron, Thane – you know what that means.'

'As good as an anti-personnel bomb,' said Thane grimly.

'Correct. We'd kept the crowd well back as a security precaution, so they were all right – just minor cuts and fainting women. There's damage, but the damage that's worrying me is happening now!' Donnan groaned at the thought. 'We can't keep this one quiet – it's already going out as a news flash on radio and TV. The evening papers will be chucking everything else out of their front pages, not just here but over most of Europe. I've had the Home Secretary, the Foreign Secretary, my own bosses, even the ruddy Post Office, all jumping on me and asking what I'm doing about it. By tonight the propaganda machines will have started grinding on the other side of the Curtain, and who'll be left holding the baby? Me!'

Thane made a sympathetic noise. 'Think it was a time bomb?'

'No. Too accurate for that. Shashkov arrived five minutes late, yet it still popped off exactly as he drove past. The army bomb disposal types are still there, but they're betting on some type of short-range radio control. We've got one lead – a beat man, one of the squad on crowd control, says he remembers noticing a small parcel being shoved in the slot of the mail box by a man who drove up in a grey Ford Zephyr. The cordon boys were just arriving for duty, it was almost a couple of hours before Shashkov was due, and he thought nothing of it at the time.'

'Any description?'

'Medium height, raincoat – that's all.' Donnan paused hopefully. 'The car wouldn't mean anything to you, would it?'

'Not a thing.' Thane shrugged at his second-in-command.

'Well, it was just a long shot. For what it's worth, there's

76

a priority warning going out to all forces. But we've no registration number for the car, and we can't throw the driver of every grey Zephyr into jug just so that we can sort things out.' An even more bitter note crept into his voice. 'The only person who isn't worried is Shashkov. Last time I saw him he growled like a bear – then grinned when he thought I wasn't watching. Probably thinks that being on the receiving end of an imperialist-type plot will give his popularity a big boost back home. But look, Thane, there's always a chance this car could be heading north –'

'We'll do our best,' Thane assured him, then hung up after Donnan had said a mournful goodbye. The unattended switchboard was already buzzing like an angry bee, with four calls waiting to be answered, two of them showing angrily flashing signal discs. He opened the door and the shopkeeper's wife hurried back to duty.

Kelch and Serviev, Stender and Bretsun – still on the loose, probably with another plan ready to put into action once they learned their second bid had failed . . .

'Well, as I always say, third time lucky,' said the woman by his side.

'Eh?' He blinked.

'Mrs MacDonald in the village.' She connected the last of the waiting calls and sat back. 'She's just had a son, and her with two daughters before him – her sister was on the line just now.'

'Nice for her – the mother, I mean,' said Thane absently. 'Phil, you heard most of Donnan?'

'Enough.' Moss gave a wince of unrelated pain. His ulcer was stirring, as it always did when the going was early and rough. He felt it grumble again and reached into one pocket of his worn tweed jacket, seeking the little pill-box he'd been nursing for just such an emergency.

'Not much we can do except keep on our own course.' Thane watched half-interestedly as his second-in-command swallowed one of the little yellow tablets from the box. 'What the heck are these?'

'A sample box of new stuff my doctor wants me to try out. Activated' – Moss frowned his way through the wording on the pill-box label – 'activated methylpolysiloxane. Well, whatever it is, it can't do much harm. What about this trunk call list?'

'Let's see it.' The Millside chief skimmed over the entries for Lady Dunspar's number. 'Kelch reached her last Friday night – there's a call to Glasgow listed, then another to the same number the following morning, followed by two to somewhere in Perth. What's this one?' He showed the book to the grocer's wife, who was still at the switchboard.

'A telegram, Mr Thane.'

'Got a copy handy?'

She shook her head. 'For telegrams, I just put the caller through to Dunkeld. They'll have it there.'

He checked through the rest of the list, but after the Saturday it seemed Lady Dunspar had had no more need of trunk telephone conversations.

'Phil, get on to Information and dig up names and addresses for these numbers – then try and find out what was in that telegram.' He gave the woman a chance to handle Moss's call and deal with a couple of waiting village subscribers, then asked her, 'Any way of knowing details about local calls made from Lady Dunspar's phone?'

'No.' She saw his disappointment and relented. 'Well, not officially, if you know what I mean. But in a wee place like this you soon get a fair idea of the numbers people will call regularly. And I can usually remember if they've asked for anyone out of the ordinary, like the minister or the doctor.'

It was a slender hope, but Thane grabbed for it. 'How about Lady Dunspar, then? Think hard – it's important.'

The grocer's wife frowned in an effort of concentration.

78

'No, she didn't have the doctor – that was Mrs Douglas, with her breathlessness. Wait now' – she gave a snap of her fingers – 'yes, she wanted one of the garages in Dunkeld.'

'When? What day?'

'I'm trying.' She frowned again. 'First thing on Sunday morning, that was it. Aye, I'm sure now, because I kept on ringing for a solid three minutes before they answered. With most folk, I'd simply have told them there was no reply. But with Lady Dunspar, it's different.' The grocer's wife toyed with the board's plug lines, a frown gathering. 'She's not in trouble herself is she – I mean, with you asking all these questions about her?'

Thane shook his head. 'Don't worry about it. And don't talk about it either, if you really want to help her. Now, can you remember which garage she telephoned?'

She had flushed a little. 'Och, it was young Tommy Harton's place. That's why she had to wait so long for an answer – he's on there by himself on a Sunday, and he never gets out of bed on time.'

Sunday morning and a garage – it added up, added up all too well. 'How do I get there?'

'Straight along the Dunkeld road for about two miles, and you can't miss it,' she assured him.

He was ready to go, but Phil Moss was still apparently tied to the telephone, his expression and the irate snap in his voice as he talked to the unfortunate at the other end of the line showing that all wasn't going smoothly.

'Trouble, Phil?'

'Trouble?' Moss clasped his hand over the instrument's mouthpiece. 'I've been shuffled between three operators up till now, but the one I've got right now seems more or less intelligent. Why? Going somewhere?'

Thane explained then left him to resume the battle and went out of the little store. The drive from there to the garage coincided with a pattering of rain on the Jaguar's roof as the first fringe of a menacing bank of heavy, dark

79

cloud began coming in from the west. The driver had to switch on the car's wipers just before they reached their destination.

Harton's Garage consisted of two petrol pumps, a little wooden hut used as an office and, at the rear, a brick-built repair shop and garage area new enough to still have only primer paint over the wood of the door-frames. The office hut was empty but, his coat collar turned up against the increasing downpour, Thane crossed over to the repair shop.

'Petrol, mister?' A young, freckle-faced mechanic left the tyre he'd been repairing and came towards him.

'I'm looking for Tommy Harton.' Thane told him, glancing over to where two older men were wrestling with the innards of a mud-spattered tractor.

'That's me.' The youngster grinned. 'If you've got car trouble –'

Thane shook his head. 'Police.'

'Oh!' Harton pulled a rag from his overall pocket, wiped his hands, and jerked his head in the direction of the hut. 'If it's private, we'd better go into the office.'

Thane followed him out through the rain and into the little building. An untidy collection of letters, forms and other papers on the table within reminded him for a moment of his own desk back at Millside. There were two chairs, an unlit stove, and the rest of the area was occupied by cartons of vehicle spares.

'Fag?' Harton offered his battered packet, took one after Thane, and accepted a light. 'What's the trouble?'

'You had a telephone call on Sunday morning from Lady Dunspar.' Thane drew on the cigarette, watching the youngster's face. 'I'd like to know what she wanted.'

'Why?' Harton made it a challenge.

'Because I'm interested.'

The youngster shook his head. 'Sorry, that's not good enough. This place is mine, mister – but I don't hide it from anybody that the reason is she gave me a help to get going, the kind of help banks don't give you unless you give them the kind of security that shows you don't need the money anyway.' He swept a place clear on the table and perched himself on the edge, waiting.

Thane took a gamble. 'She telephoned about a car, didn't she – a grey Ford Zephyr?' The youngster's slightly tightened expression was answer enough. 'Keep quiet if you want, Harton. Nobody can force you to co-operate, but you're only heading into a mess of trouble. I'm not trying to nail a charge on the woman, but I may have to unless I find someone who'll give me some sensible answers.'

'How . . . how serious is it?'

'Among other things, murder.' The words came hard and cold from Thane's lips. 'Is that enough?'

Harton swallowed and nodded. 'All right – if you mean it about her not being involved. She phoned here on Sunday, about a car.'

'Whose car is it?'

'Mine.' Harton came off the table, went over to the stove, and flipped his half-smoked cigarette into the open front. 'She has a car of her own, but her daughter has been using it most of the time, and she lives away from home. When Lady Dunspar rang me, she said she needed some form of transport right away, for a few days. Some friends had arrived, and she wanted to drive them around.' He shrugged. 'Well, I helped out.'

'And gave her the Ford.'

'Why not?' demanded Harton defensively. 'She did me a good turn. The Ford's mine, and I told her she could have a loan of it till today.'

'You mean' – it was Thane's turn to be surprised – 'you mean you've got it back?'

'Not yet,' said the youngster patiently. 'Look, I need the car tonight. I'm hiring it out to a Yank who's coming up for the fishing, and he's due to arrive in Dunkeld this evening. I've got the letter he sent . . .' He began to paw through the papers on the table.

'Never mind it,' snapped Thane. 'What's the arrange-ment for returning the car?'

'I'm collecting it from her home this afternoon.' Harton scratched his head. 'When I gave her the Ford I told her I'd need it back today, and that I'd fix up something else to take its place. I'm giving her an old Austin, not as good a car, but the only thing I've got available.'

'I don't think she'll need it somehow.' Thane pursed his lips. 'What's the Ford's registration number?'

'608 XMG, but –'

Colin Thane was already on his way to the car outside. A moment later, as it sped back through the rain towards the grocery store and Phil Moss, he was calling control on the Jaguar's radio. The control operator's voice answered, faint but distinct, giving him a strength three reading.

He flicked the 'send' switch again. 'Add to special search message and with direct advice to Colonel Donnan through Edinburgh city headquarters . . .' He passed on the Ford's number, had it acknowledged, and moments later heard the girl putting out the message on the general net.

Phil Moss was lounging in the doorway of the village store, sheltering from the last drops of the fading rain-storm. Thane threw open the car's rear door as it braked to a halt alongside.

'Get in – quick.'

Moss tumbled aboard and slammed the door as the car began rolling again, tyres hissing on the wet road.

'Colin, I've –'

'We're heading back to Lady Dunspar's place,' Thane cut across him. 'That grey Ford, Phil. She borrowed it from a local garage, and it's due to be returned this afternoon.'

Moss blinked. 'And I thought I had news! I traced the call she made to Glasgow on the Friday evening. She telephoned Peter Herrald, his number anyway.' He gave a bitter grimace of satisfaction. 'The other thing is I can tell you where I saw the girl before –'

'What girl?' Thane growled it, still trying to absorb the implication of a link to the missing angler.

'The girl in the painting in her house. It was the dark hair that threw me – but Herrald's name triggered it. She may be Lady Dunspar's daughter, but her hair is blonde now and she calls herself Barbara Mason.'

'The hotel receptionist you spoke to – Herrald's girl friend!'

'The same.' Moss grabbed for support as the car swung round the next corner, the back end sliding first one way then the other as the driver calmly controlled the skid. 'What's the rush? You don't imagine these boys are going to be kind and considerate enough to bring the old girl her car back the way they promised, do you?'

'I'd do it, Phil – make a point of it, in fact. Look, Kelch is no fool. His bunch have been using a car which in theory is out on loan to a quiet, elderly woman. It wouldn't be easy to trace back unless somebody managed to catch the registration number.'

'And they may have false plates rigged,' admitted Moss.

'Right. Still, Kelch won't want to hang on to the one car for too long, and bringing the Ford back gives them an equally easy chance to switch cars – leaving everybody looking for a grey Ford while they're actually running around in another car which nobody is going to report as being either stolen or hired!'

He'd satisfied Moss, and now, as the car rushed on, Thane had a puzzle of his own . . . Herrald and Lady Dunspar's daughter. 'Phil, what about the other phone calls, and that telegram?'

'The two Perth calls were to her bank, the Central Scottish. The telegram was to a woman friend on the other side of Dunkeld telling her she couldn't keep a date they had for the Sunday.' Moss winced as the Jaguar flirted round another corner on the thickly hedged road and glanced anxiously towards the speedometer. 'Do we have to go so fast right now?'

A faint smile suppressed in the corners of his mouth, their driver took a fraction of pressure off the accelerator but Thane nodded him on again.

'We do. It's only a two-hour drive from Edinburgh to this part of the world. If the Ford left the city soon after the bombing, it should be getting pretty close to us right now. And we've got to get it, Phil. We've got to get whoever is in it.'

Four men, three, two, one – just as long as he had one of the group, a chance to lay his hands on something or somebody at the heart of the situation, somebody or something more tangible than the present maze of half-innocent helpers who seemed to surround Kelch's every move. Thane stared along the road ahead, the rain drumming louder on the car roof, the wipers sweeping their regular beat.

The car's radio came to life at the same instant as the red roof of Lady Dunspar's home appeared in the distance ahead. He grabbed the microphone and acknowledged.

'Glasgow car one-eleven, Chief Inspector Thane.' The merest fraction of a pause as the girl operator drew breath, and then she went on, 'Grey Ford 608 XMG reported seen heading north on the main A9 road near Bankfoot, one occupant. Report is from Bankfoot constable and traffic car six-two is heading south on A9 to intercept. Over.'

'Roger. Also in area and closing. Out.' Thane tossed the microphone into its cubbyhole. 'Phil?'

His second-in-command already had the map unfolded. 'He could branch off for here about three miles north of Bankfoot.'

'How far from here to the junction?'

'Maybe another three. Unless the traffic car gets him, he should be heading straight for us.'

As the Jaguar whipped past the red-roofed villa, their

84

driver glanced at them through his mirror. 'Do I keep going, sir, or do you want to block him?'

Thane chewed his lower lip. Nine chances out of ten the Ford was coming their way. But there was the tenth chance, and only one other mobile unit in the area. 'Keep going, but be ready for trouble,' he ordered. 'He's liable to try anything, but stop the car any way you can – I'll carry the can if the result is a pile-up.'

They'd topped a slight rise and were notching seventy down the long straight of the reverse slope, down to where a smaller service road branched off to the right, when they saw the Ford. The grey car, a rain-distorted blur at first, was driving towards them at a more sedate pace but the first sign of the approaching Jaguar seemed to warn the other driver. The Ford slowed then accelerated violently, tackling a slithering, tyre-screaming turn which shot it into the side road.

'Take him.'

The two Millside men grabbed for support as their driver obeyed.

Six cylinders, over three and a half litres of engine, bellowed as the car dropped down a gear for maximum acceleration and jerked forward. The uniformed figure at the wheel settled into a tight-shouldered crouch, half-crooning as he coaxed the 220 brake horsepower of the sleek projectile under his control. They took the branch road's angle in a bounding slide, and the car stayed in third gear until every last safe rev. had been pulled from its power unit.

The Ford ahead was moving fast and being handled well over the narrow, hedge-lined service road – but Thane's car had a full litre of engine advantage, controlled by a professional.

The grey car reached a wheel-hopping, desperate pace yet the gap between them closed with such a rush that its pursuer had to ease up to avoid nosing into its rear.

'Road's too narrow, sir,' reported Thane's driver, letting

the gap widen again. 'Corner ahead – once we're round it I'll try giving him a nudge.'

The Ford's driver looked back at them once before the corner, a quick, jerking glance before he wrestled the grey car into a wildly braking turn which spelled torture for suspension and transmission. Rubber screamed again, then as the car's tail disappeared from view there was a sudden thunder of impacting metal and shattered glass. As the Jaguar slithered to a skidding, brake-singing halt Thane had a momentary glimpse of a round black object hurtling skywards. Then he was being jerked forward in his seat, Phil Moss thrown against him as their car came to a final halt, angled across the roadway and half-distance round the corner.

'Hell, he's really copped it, sir!' Their driver spoke with awe, shaken at their own narrow escape.

A few yards ahead, the crumpled wreck of the grey car was almost wrapped round what had once been a farm tractor but was now an equally twisted tangle of metal. The savage impact on the wet surface had swept both vehicles off the road and tumbled them sideways into the deep drainage ditch which ran a few feet in from the verge. One of the Ford's front wheels was still spinning, the other, the wheel Thane had seen going into the air as it was torn loose, lay about twenty yards further on.

'There's someone –' Moss threw open the car's door and they scrambled out into the steady downpour as a man struggled to his feet on the opposite side of the road from the wreckage. He staggered and almost fell again as they reached him, the glaze of pure shock still in his eyes.

'Came straight at me, man – straight at the tractor . . .' the farm worker's limbs trembled jerkily, '. . . I jumped for it. Straight at me, he was comin'.'

The two policemen left him to the driver's care and sprinted over to the Ford. The rain spattered and hissed against the car's exposed exhaust as Thane clambered on to the tilted side and managed to wrench open the buckled metal of the driver's door. He threw it back, looked inside the car and felt sick. Stocky build, medium height, age about forty, close-cropped grey hair and a small moustache – the description tallied with the one Colonel Donnan had passed on.

But Taras Serviev was both trapped and dying. The steering wheel had taken him in the chest, glass splinters had drawn blood from half a dozen cuts on his face and hands and his legs were pinned beneath the shattered engine bulkhead, leaving him lying at an angle against the wide bench seat.

The man's head turned slowly, painfully, and his lips parted in an attempt at a cynical welcome. Thane pulled himself into a better position and nodded to Moss. 'We'll need help, Phil – ambulance and a breakdown crew.' While Moss sprinted back through the rain towards the Jaguar, he eased his head and shoulders inside the wreckage. 'It won't take long, Serviev.'

'Any time . . . too long.' Serviev gave a faint shake of his head. 'You . . . know me?'

Thane nodded. 'And the others. Where are they, Serviev? Where's Kelch?'

The trapped man moistened his lips. 'Cigarette . . .'

Thane sniffed the reek of petrol in the air and shook his head. 'Too risky.'

'Life is . . . risk.' Serviev tried to move, and gave a moaning gasp of pain.

Thane eased himself still closer. 'Serviev, where's Martin Kelch? And where's Peter Herrald – what's happened to him?'

'Safe.' The trapped man drew a wheezing, shallow breath. 'Shashkov will . . . die before you . . . find.' He seemed to come close to losing his slender grip on consciousness, then drew on some last source of energy and looked up again. He ran his tongue over his lips and gave a bare-toothed grimace. 'Drink . . .'

'All right.' Thane raised himself up and saw Phil Moss

coming back from the Jaguar. 'Phil, can you find some water?'

'Water.' Moss brushed the trickles of rain from his face and gave a gloomy nod. He went back to the police car and returned in a moment carrying the water bottle from the emergency kit.

'Thanks.' Thane unscrewed the cap, gripped the bottle with his right hand and eased back into the wreck. 'Here it is, Serviev.'

As the water touched his lips, Serviev tried to swallow. His eyes met Thane's and he struggled to speak for a moment.

'Take your time.' The Millside chief leaned still further forward as Serviev tried to reach up with one hand. 'Just sip – I'll worry about the bottle.'

'Bottle . . .' Serviev twitched and he stared at Thane. Then suddenly his face twisted into the start of a laugh, a strangely taunting laugh. 'You . . .'

He died before the chuckle had been more than shaped on his lips. Thane waited a moment, then climbed back down from the wreckage. As he did, he became freshly aware of the beating rain, the cold wet feel of the metal on which he'd been lying, the way the rivulets of water ran down the front of his coat, soaking into the damp, clinging cloth.

One accounted for – but three to go, plus Peter Herrald still to be found. And all he'd learned towards that was that Herrald was alive.

He was still standing by the wreck when the county traffic car arrived. Another twenty minutes went by before the ambulance and breakdown truck reached the scene.

# Chapter Five

It was mid-afternoon before Thane paid his second call on Lady Dunspar. When he arrived, a small blue-and-white Triumph coupé was parked on the driveway and the front door was opened by a girl whom he knew immediately. Phil Moss had been right. Accept that the dark hair had been dyed blonde, that a pretty school-child develops into an attractive woman, and Lady Dunspar's daughter hadn't really changed too much since her portrait had been painted.

'Come in, please, Chief Inspector.' Barbara Mason was slim, smaller than her mother, neat in waist and bust, dressed in a sheath dress of dark grey jersey wool. Her eyes were a hazel brown and worried, her voice had the neutral warmth of the trained receptionist. She closed the door once he'd entered, then showed him into the lounge. Lady Dunspar sat by the fireside, the small table next to her chair set for afternoon tea . . . and she'd changed from her gardening clothes into a plain, expensively tailored navy blue costume.

'You're alone, Chief Inspector?' She motioned him to the chair opposite while her daughter hovered restlessly in the background. 'Barbara, is this . . .?'

'No, it was another one,' said the girl cautiously. 'I can't remember his name.'

'Detective Inspector Moss,' Thane told her. 'He was with me this morning, when we came to see your mother. But we didn't link you with her until later.'

89

'I'm a widow, Chief Inspector.' She gave the wedding ring on her left hand a nervous twist. 'My husband's name was Mason.'

'And let me save a little of your time, Mr Thane.' Lady Dunspar's voice was quiet and steady. 'Barbara knows why you were here. In return, she told me something I didn't know this morning. You said a man called Shaw had been killed. But you didn't tell me that his companion – the man who disappeared – was named Herrald. That might have made a difference.'

Thane nodded. 'He's still missing, Lady Dunspar – the same Peter Herrald you telephoned on Friday evening.' He saw her surprise and gave a tight smile. 'It's my turn to say that was something I didn't know this morning. But a lot has happened since. For a start, you're wondering why a certain car wasn't returned on schedule, aren't you?'

The two women exchanged glances, then Lady Dunspar gave a soft sigh. 'You've discovered quite a lot in a very short time, Mr Thane. I suppose I should congratulate you.'

He was fairly certain now that they were going to talk, but it was a moment for shock tactics, a final blow to smash any remaining reluctance. 'The car crashed about two hours ago, during a chase on a farm road not far from here. The driver died.' As the colour ebbed from her face he shook his head. 'Martin Kelch wasn't aboard. The driver's name was Serviev – he was responsible for a bomb explosion in Edinburgh this morning, an explosion just as General Shashkov was arriving at a factory.'

'Was he –'

'Killed? No, Shashkov's all right. But there are five other men in hospital, at least one critically ill. Policemen, Lady Dunspar. One of their jobs was to hold back the crowd that had gathered . . . a crowd of men, women, children.' His words came flat and level, yet were eloquent in their muted anger. 'Your opinion may be different. But for my money anyone who'll explode a bomb like the one this morning rates as a mad dog, and no matter how fond you've been of a dog, when he goes mad he has to be hunted down.'

There was pain as well as dignity in her nod. 'I understand.'

'Good.' Thane looked at mother and daughter in turn. 'I came here alone for a reason. Down in England one policeman's evidence of what he sees or hears is enough on its own. But not in Scotland – up here, any statement must have two witnesses. In other words, if you answer my questions I can use the information. But because I'm alone, I couldn't prove in court that you'd said a word. I thought you might find that – well, easier.'

'What you really mean is that you'll learn more from me if I'm not worried about being dragged off to a cell in the local police station.' Lady Dunspar showed a brief twinkle of her more usual humour. 'Barbara' – she beckoned her daughter forward – 'Mr Thane might like some tea while we talk.'

'You're sure, Mother?' The girl crossed over and laid a hand on her mother's shoulder. She bit her lip. 'It's your decision, but –'

'It's my decision.' Lady Dunspar was firm. 'Just one thing, Mr Thane. Barbara at no time played any part in what has happened . . . at no time.'

'Then why did she come here?' Thane watched the blonde hotel receptionist pour tea into the cups. 'Why this afternoon?'

'I'll answer for myself.' The girl jerked round. 'Yesterday I was questioned about Peter – no reasons given, just asked if I knew where he was, how long I'd known him, other things. Then this morning I discovered I was being followed, and not very cleverly, Mr Thane. Well, I knew Peter had been planning a fishing holiday near here with a friend called Shaw. So I dodged my policeman and drove up to find out if my mother knew anything about what was happening.' She turned back to the cups. 'Sugar?'

'Thanks.' Thane rubbed his chin. 'Couldn't you have telephoned?'

'I once operated a hotel switchboard.' She handed him his cup. 'I've never felt quite the same about telephones since.'

Thane gave in. 'All right. Supposing we start at the beginning – with Peter Herrald.'

It was one of the strangest interviews he'd ever coped with, sitting there balancing the delicate Royal Doulton cup and saucer on his knee, refusing a biscuit, nodding as Lady Dunspar answered his questions, her daughter coming in occasionally to supplement the older woman's replies.

Barbara Mason and Peter Herrald had met at a party in Glasgow about two months before and Herrald, whose business apparently left him with both time and a reasonable amount of money to spare, had begun dating her regularly. On the third week, a drive north into the Highlands had ended in their visiting Lady Dunspar – and they'd been back at the house together twice more since then.

'A close friendship?'

'We weren't in love, if that's what you mean.' The young widow flushed. 'We liked each other's company, but that's as far as it went. I'm not hunting for a new husband – and Peter liked coming here, even though most of the time Mother kept telling him about the work she'd done at that refugee camp.'

'He was interested in it,' protested Lady Dunspar. 'In a way, that's why all this has happened – why I'm to blame.' She set down the cup, her manner weary. 'You see, I told him about Martin. Martin always wanted to go abroad, Mr Thane. But it wasn't always easy for refugees, and he couldn't get the necessary permissions . . . if he had, he wouldn't have gone back to his own country.'

The rest of the sequence fell into place. Herrald had listened and sympathized. He'd talked about his own interests, the import-export contacts which were part of his business, his nodding acquaintance with Glasgow's sprawling dockland.

'And that's why –'

'Why I thought of him when Martin arrived here needing help,' nodded Lady Dunspar.

Thane listened. She'd telephoned Peter Herrald at his home on the Friday evening, asking if he knew any way in which the four runaway trawlermen could be got aboard a ship towards their goal.

'He said he wasn't sure, but that he'd certainly do what he could – then he told me he was coming north anyway, and that the best idea might be for him to meet Martin and the others.'

'You telephoned him again the next morning?'

'Yes. Martin had been worried about the idea, but he'd agreed by then. He spoke to Peter, and they arranged a meeting for the Tuesday.'

'Where? At the old cottage?'

She shook her head. 'No. It was to be at Aberfeldy, in the evening.'

'Did your guests know about General Shashkov's visit by then?'

'Yes. I – I told Martin myself. I don't know why, I just – just thought it was something that would interest him.'

'It looks as though it did,' said Thane, his expression grim. 'How did they react?'

'They were bitter.' Lady Dunspar looked up at him. 'Yes, especially Martin, Chief Inspector – people who have suffered have a right to their feelings. But these men were only interested in getting away, getting right out of Europe. Not one of them hinted at anything else.'

It was after Herrald's call that she'd first suggested the old cottage as a hideout. Then she'd despatched a shaved, cleaned-up Kelch into Perth carrying a cheque drawn on her bank – telephoning first to make sure it would be cashed on the spot, then again to satisfy herself there had been no hitch. By the time he'd returned, the three other trawlermen had helped her lay out a stock of tinned food from her own household stores.

'The car came last, of course,' she told Thane. 'I knew young Tommy Harton would give me one, but I thought leaving it till the last minute looked more natural.'

'When did they leave?'

'A little before noon on Sunday, and I haven't seen them since.' She held her head high. 'That's my story, Mr Thane.'

He swung towards her daughter. 'And you knew nothing about any of this – Herrald didn't call you to tell you what was happening?'

The girl shook her head. 'Neither Peter nor my mother wanted me to be involved – she told me nothing until today.' She took a cigarette from a box on the table, lit it with a quick, nervous snap of the matching table lighter, and asked, 'What do you think has happened to him? Do you . . . do you think he's been killed too?'

'Not according to Serviev. About the only thing he did tell me was that Herrald was safe.' Thane shrugged. 'We won't really know until we've found him.' Another point still puzzled him. 'Lady Dunspar, why did you believe that Kelch couldn't have been involved in Shaw's death if it had happened on Wednesday?'

She kneaded her fingers together on her lap. 'Because Martin telephoned here on Tuesday night. He said he was going with Peter Herrald to Glasgow the next morning, and that it looked as if their troubles were just about over.'

'Anything else?'

She said no. Patiently, Thane back-tracked over the story, seeking any possible lead to where Kelch and his companions might have gone to once they had to leave the cottage. He drew a blank. No, they'd left nothing behind them – he was welcome to search if he chose, and no need for a warrant. No, there had been no further contact since the Tuesday call – she'd been hoping that Martin Kelch himself might return for the change-over of cars and she could have found out what had happened.

'One last point.' Thane plugged on patiently. 'When Kelch was a refugee over here, did he know anyone from the Stirling area?'

'I suppose so.' She frowned. 'It's possible. He was given a job working in a coal mine – a lot of the refugees got the chance. But like most of them, his health didn't stand up to it.'

'Flenders Colliery?'

She concentrated for a moment. 'I think that was the name. Why?'

Routine, he told her. Barbara Mason showed him out, her mother sitting in the chair beside the Adam fireplace, a hurt, bewildered look on her face.

'Will you be back?' The young blonde widow's manner made it plain she hoped for a negative answer.

'Probably.'

'I suppose you'll have men watching here.' Her face was tight and angry.

'They started just before you arrived, Mrs Mason.'

She paused at the doorway and looked out across the green of the grass towards the river. 'My mother doesn't go in for emotional scenes, Chief Inspector. You heard her say she blames herself for most of this. If Peter – if he's dead, she'll feel that's her fault too.' She shrugged. 'I don't suppose it matters – the police don't trust anyone very much, do they?'

'Goodbye, Mrs Mason.' He said nothing more, though he was tempted. The door slammed shut, and he walked back down the driveway to his ear.

The arranged rendezvous was back at Aberfeldy, and he arrived there at an awkward moment – Phil Moss and Colonel Donnan stood inside the main office of the little police station, Donnan flushed and angry, Moss with a stubborn, determined glower on his thin, lined face. In the background, one of the local police was self-consciously fixing his attention on writing a report.

The sudden silence as he entered was warning enough. Thane looked from one man to the other and sighed. 'All right, what's up?'

The two men bristled, each waiting for the other to speak.

'Visitors first, then,' declared Thane. 'Colonel?'

The little Irishman drew himself erect. 'I've half a mind' – he ignored the quick, cynical twist which glinted on his opponent's lips – 'I've half a mind to report him for insubordination, insulting language and . . .'

'And commonsense,' suggested Moss acidly.

Thane threw a frown towards him. 'Quiet, Phil – you'll have your turn.'

Moss shrugged. 'Sorry.'

'What was the trouble, Colonel?'

Donnan scowled. 'I come galloping up here as soon as I hear about Serviev's crash. Then Moss tells me about the link between Herrald and Lady Dunspar's daughter – yet when I ask him to have Glasgow police pick her up for requestioning he gives me a flat refusal. I make a second request – that he turns over to me any papers found on Serviev – and again he refuses.'

'What about the insulting language?' proved Thane.

'Well . . .' Donnan pursed his lips. 'Maybe there was some on both sides. But nobody calls me a – a bog-trotting Mick and gets away with it.'

'Barbara Mason is with her mother – I've just come from talking to them both,' said Thane. 'Anyway, I'd have turned down your idea. Some people you pull in, and they talk. Others you get more from by leaving them to think things over. Her mother admits contacting Herrald and asking him to help, but says the girl knew nothing – I'm

96

inclined to believe her. She also says Martin Kelch once worked at Flenders Colliery.'

'Where the explosives were stolen!' Donnan temporarily forgot his feud. 'That explains one part of the puzzle.' Then he scowled again, though not quite so angrily. 'There are still these papers . . .'

'Serviev's pockets were empty,' said Thane.

Moss cleared his throat. 'Colin, we did find a couple things in the car, after you'd gone. They were under the front seat. I thought you'd better see 'em first, before they . . . disappeared. They've been checked for prints. Negative apart from Serviev.' He turned to a paper-wrapped bundle on the table at his side. 'Ever seen one of these?'

Thane took the small, metal-framed box and examined it. A factory-made unit, fairly similar to the speed control unit on his youngster's electric train set, it was different in that there were no outlet terminals, only a small socket at one end and a single, calibrated knob.

'I have,' said Donnan. 'It's a remote control unit for one of those fancy toy speedboats. The box is an elementary short-range transmitter – its signal varies the boat's rudder control. Well, the idea's simple enough – the bomb disposal boys found some fragments in the letter-box wreckage which were probably the other end of the system.'

Buy the two sections of the remote control in a toyshop, fit one into a package with gelignite and an electrically fired detonator, the electric circuit completed when the rudder control was swung by the transmitter's action, the transmitter operator a safe distance away . . . they saw now how the blast could have been so perfectly timed by men who had had only a few days and limited resources available to rig a package of potential death.

'What else?' Thane leaned over the table, his curiosity mounting.

Moss flipped a golf tee along the table. The little wooden shape spun to a gradual halt as he lifted out the last of his finds. 'The tee was jammed under the carpeting, as if it had fallen from somebody's pocket. But this little piece of work was tied under the seat springs, held so that it would stay nice and handy.'

The knife had a six-inch blade, the steel stone-honed down to half its original thickness, a needle point backed by two razor-keen edges. Thane ran his thumb lightly along the cold metal. It didn't take much imagination to realize how effective a weapon it would have been. He'd seen knives like it before, but used for a more peaceful purpose. 'Once upon a time this was a fish-gutting knife, Phil. Most deep-sea fishermen have one – but not worked into this fashion.'

'It's still a gutting knife,' agreed Donnan soberly. 'But not for fish, Thane.' He turned to Phil Moss, a grudging respect back in his eyes. 'Well, if Ketch and his men are still in business tomorrow, that golf tee tells us where they're going to make their next try.'

'The Old Course?'

'At St. Andrews,' nodded the security man. 'Can I have the transmitter box now? I'd like the Army bomb disposal people to see it. They may be able to rig some sort of jamming device.'

'It's an idea,' agreed Thane. 'If Kelch has another little package ready, the same as today's, it would give him quite a surprise if you jammed the wavelength, maybe even caused a premature bang. But where could he plant the bomb this time?'

'Your guess is as good as mine.' Donnan shrugged. 'The course is closed for all play tomorrow until General Shashkov has completed his round. Every step he takes he'll be covered by a security screen. I've got cops, some of my own men, a bunch of R.A.F. police drafted over from Leuchars air station – and precautions will be stiffer than ever after today. I'd like to see him cancel the rest of his programme, but the old devil's insisting on carrying it out to the letter, and saying it is up to us to keep him in one piece. He's almost enjoying the situation.'

'Will he have a gallery following him around?'

'Bound to have – and a big one. Maybe several hundred people.' Colonel Donnan's unhappiness was complete. 'We can keep them fairly well back, outside ropes. The stewards and the guard force have orders that only a picked entourage group of reporters and camera-men get inside the cordon. But we can't do more. If we sealed the course off from the outside world it would be an admission of complete and absolute ruddy fright, and Moscow's propaganda factories would make us look like a bunch of red-nosed comics – that, or blood-stained capitalistic lackies keeping the Soviet's hero isolated from making friendly contact with the eager, downtrodden Scottish peasantry.'

'You've a fair grasp of the language,' Thane told him. 'What's he like anyway?'

'The lingo is infectious when part of your daily chore is reading translated extracts from *Pravda* to find out which way the wind's blowing,' grunted Donnan. 'Shashkov? He's one of the bunch who grabbed their chance when Joe Stalin's day ended. Tough as nails – though he's supposed to be out of favour with some sections of the Moscow clique, who think he's wearing the velvet gloves too often nowadays. He's one of the divide and conquer brigade, strictly a Cold War merchant with sense enough to know his side would get just as hurt as anyone if the cold ever turned to hot.'

'Better the de'il you know than the de'il you don't,' mused Thane, laying the knife back in the parcel then reaching in again to take out a folded newspaper which had been lying at its foot. 'What about this, Phil?'

'It was in the glove compartment. Yesterday's edition of the *Bugle* – I looked through it, but there's no marking of any kind.' Moss stuck his hands in his pockets. 'Still, I thought I'd better leave it with the rest.'

'Made any arrangements about Serviev's clothing?'

'A car's bringing the stuff from the mortuary.'

Thane glanced at his watch. Behind them, the local

constable had finished writing his report and had lit a cigarette. 'Well, there doesn't seem to be much else we can do around here. Unless – you said you had a complaint to lodge, Colonel. Want to make it official?'

'Oh, the hell with it.' The little security man grinned. 'I've got the jitters, that's all – anyone seems to be rubbing me the wrong way, and I react.'

'It could be a potential ulcer.' Thane's eyes twinkled with a mixture of humour and relief. 'Ask Moss – he's an authority. But not now. You're going back to Shashkov?'

'As usual. This is the night he eats with the Secretary of State.' Colonel Donnan shook his head. 'The way things are going, they'll want me to taste the soup before it's served.'

Thane had already given the security man his ration of sympathy. 'Have fun,' he nodded. 'Phil, I want you to go over to St. Andrews. Say hello to the local police, then start asking around the Old Course staff – starter, greenkeepers, ticket rangers, anyone like that. If that golf tee means what we think, then Kelch or Serviev or one of the others has been recce-ing that golf course. Better try the local golf equipment shops too. With Lady Dunspar's money in their pockets, plus what they took from Herrald's office, they'd be able to outfit themselves for the game.'

'Hotels have already been checked,' contributed Colonel Donnan. 'We drew a blank. But – no, we didn't inquire too closely on casual golfers. The Old Course is public, pay your money and play your game – there must be scores of players going over it every day.'

'Then we'll just have to hope that our trawlermen were spectacular enough to be remembered.' Thane bundled the package together, pushing the control device towards Donnan. 'I'm taking these and Serviev's clothing back to Glasgow, to let Dan Laurence's boffins have a look at them. He should be able to tell us more about what he found at the cottage while I'm at it . . . and with luck, I may get MacMaster's contribution at the same time.'

'Aye.' His second-in-command put an edge into the word. 'You'll be back tonight?'

'Depends on what happens, and that's up to the boffins.'

'I don't grudge you an evening at home,' said Moss with a grumble. 'That's one of the privileges of rank. I just wish you'd put more polish into the excuses.' He reached for his hat. 'I'll keep in contact with the St. Andrews station – and give Mary my love.' He had followed Donnan out of the door before Thane could muster a reply.

By early evening, Thane was back in the city. The police car had eaten distance on the long, arrow-straight dual carriageway of the new Stirling-Glasgow road, and they were travelling in past the high skyscraper flats of Glasgow's growing new skyline, the city's answer to its legacy of old, damp, rat-ridden tenement slums, at the same time as the homeward rush of end-of-day traffic was just beginning to get under way.

His driver took the car straight into the parking yard at police Headquarters, stopped, and waited hopefully.

'That's all for a spell,' nodded Thane, then thumbed towards the packages on the rear seat. 'But take these up to the Scientific Bureau before you disappear. Tell 'em I'll be along soon.'

Policy dictated his first call, on Buddha Ilford. But the city's C.I.D. boss was out. The duty man at the Central C.I.D. bar wasn't sure where or why, only that it involved a runaway bank cashier and that Chief Superintendent Ilford wouldn't be back for a couple of hours.

'You know the old man,' he winked. 'Every now and again he gets off his backside, takes over a job, and goes out into the big, bad world.'

Thane had experienced it before. Buddha's brief excursions back to working detection formed a type of safety valve, one the C.I.D. boss claimed helped keep him sane in the face of his usual round of desk-bound activities. Some-times, though, the disappearance could be awkward for the divisional men. Either they were looking for him in a hurry, or Buddha would turn up out of the blue and catch them on the hop.

'When he comes in, I'd like to know.'

'You will.' The duty man turned back to monitor the radio, which was beginning to brisken with messages to the mobile units. As Thane left, the first of the night shift squads were beginning to drift in . . . Friday night was pay night, and they'd have a busy evening once the pubs closed at 9.30 and their customers scattered around the streets.

'Chief Inspector . . .' The hail came as he crossed the street again to the main Headquarters building. He slowed to let the hurrying figure of Detective Sergeant MacLeod catch up with him. The Millside sergeant puffed a little after his sprint. 'Didn't expect to see you here, sir!'

'Makes a change from chasing my tail up north,' Thane told him. 'Anything happening in the division?'

'Nothing desperate,' said MacLeod thankfully. 'I'm along to have a word with Records office – three com-plaints of a con man working a television maintenance racket came in today, and I thought they could maybe match the method on the m.o. files and give us a lead.'

'What about Vince Bruce?'

The sergeant shook his head. The young housebreaker was still on the run. 'But brother Donny has admitted five other break-ins,' he volunteered. 'We've recovered some of the stuff.'

'Donny's share?' Thane was unimpressed. 'Vince always keeps the best. He's the one I want.' He rattled the coins in his trouser pocket and remembered his other interest. 'Any word from Sam Newton?'

'Millside's pitch-and-toss expert?' MacLeod gave an involuntary twinkle. 'Aye, he phoned in. He's made contact with some of the bunch in Jock Howard's game, and says he'll be playing tonight.'

'Good.' Constable Newton was likely to enjoy the experience of being paid to gamble. 'Tell him to stick with it – there's usually a bigger turnout on a Saturday, and then the real school get together on Sundays. If we can nail Jock Howard on a Sunday so much the better.' Thane's dry chuckle heralded misfortune for the pitch-and-toss organizer. 'Gambling on the Sabbath always looks that little bit meatier on a charge sheet.'

He said goodbye to the sergeant and went into the Headquarters building. The lift took him to the second floor, the Scientific Branch's area, branded as either hallowed or unholy precincts depending on the results produced and the effect they had on some hard-hoping divisional C.I.D. man's theories.

Dan Laurence's room was along to the left, past a showcase filled with silver cups and trophies won by the Police Athletic Association. It was a small room, tobacco-stale as usual, a bare minimum of furnishings surrounded by tottering piles of battered reference books and report files, old newspapers and unboxed equipment. Thane knocked on the opened door and went in, just as Laurence stuck his head round the connecting door leading to the main laboratory area beyond.

'It's you, is it?' The Scientific Branch chief gave a grunt. He was in his shirt-sleeves, the usual ash-tipped cigarette smouldered between his lips, its smoke making him peer through half-shut eyes. 'Hell, man, it's only ten minutes since that last load of yours was dumped on my lap.'

'I just thought I'd make sure you got it all right,' soothed Thane.

'Well, we did.' Dan Laurence was at his gruffest. 'And if characters would stop telephoning me to remind me anything connected with Martin Kelch has to have absolute priority I might have more of a chance to do something about it. Look, Colin, show some ruddy humanity – away

103

and lose yourself in the canteen, go home, go to the pictures, any damn thing, but leave us alone for a couple of hours.'

'You'll be ready by then?'

'With your stuff, yes. The lads I left up north are sending down some scrapings and fingerprint samples from the Ford your pal Serviev crashed, but it'll be nearer midnight before we've got the stuff sorted out.' He rummaged on his desk. 'Here's something while you're waiting – the report on what we got between the Mini-van and the cottage this morning.'

Thane took the half-dozen stapled sheets of close-typed quarto paper and scanned through the top page summary which gave the bare bones of the fuller detail within. When the Scientific Branch put its name to a report the apparent confusion in which they worked died into cold, carefully marshalled fact, and this one was no exception.

It started off quietly enough. Latent prints found aboard the van matched samples from Shaw's home and Herrald's flat. But there were others, still unidentified, which matched up with some of the four sets of prints each labelled 'unknown' which had been found in the cottage. Traces of Shaw's prints had also been found in the building, as had those of Herrald – or, as the Branch report stubbornly phrased it, 'were similar to fingerprints believed to be those of the men concerned.'

Next came the Mini-van. Thane raised an eyebrow. 'The bullet hole in the driver's window showed the shot had been fired from close range, at a slightly downward angle, and from outside the van . . . Dan?'

'Just what it says.' Laurence displayed his usual contempt for the non-technical mind. 'I wanted to make sure the bloke in the passenger seat didn't pull the trigger – two shots, one through the glass, the other into Shaw. But fire a bullet through glass and it punches a hole, an anything but clean hole. Put the microscope on it, and on one side there are always wee flakes o' glass blown away. The bullet is always fired from the opposite side to where the flakes are kicked loose.' The Scientific Branch chief liked his little lectures. He lit a fresh cigarette from the stub of the old and went on. 'The clean entry punch shows the bullet was fired from close up – there's a trace o' powder anyway, to tell the truth. And more flakes being punched off from the bottom o' the exit hole than the top tells us the angle. Happy?'

'Deliriously.' The last section was a report on an analysis of mud scrapings from the van's tyres and underside – local soils, stone chips, road grit, the same repeated in the dirt samples taken from the little vehicle's rubber floor mats.

'Hmm.' Laurence gazed at him quizzically. 'You're no' exactly the picture o' a satisfied customer, Colin.'

'Sorry.' Thane folded the report and put it in his pocket. 'But there's not much for me in this lot.'

'Aye, we'll maybe have better news for you when you come back,' said Laurence pointedly. 'Hey' – he snapped his fingers in sudden recollection – 'old MacMaster left a message for you. The blood on the van's seat was Group C, the same as Shaw's. Herrald's blood is Group AB. One of the Central Division lads found Herrald had his appendix taken out about a year back, and the hospital still had his card on file.'

'So Herrald should still be in one piece – Serviev said the same thing.' Thane turned towards the door, then stopped. 'Dan, I'll be back in those two hours. Anyone wants me in between, I'll either be at the *Bugle* office or at home.'

Dan Laurence shook his head as the burly Millside man went out. He liked Thane, and at that moment didn't envy him his task. But then, he didn't particularly envy any cop outside his own test-tube kingdom. Professor MacMaster's motto was that dead men could tell any amount of tales. Dan Laurence went further, and declared his laboratory could coax speech from any material.

He took the cigarette from his mouth and gave a bellow.

'Willie! Away down to the canteen and bring up some sandwiches. We've got work to do, but a man's got to eat!'

The youngest member of his team, busy at a bench in the main laboratory, heard the shout and groaned. He had a date with the little blonde policewoman who'd recently arrived on the staff down in Lost Property. He just hoped she'd understand – again.


The *Evening Bugle* office, a cream stone building which looked more like a church than the headquarters of a high-geared money-making newspaper group, was situated a stone's throw away from the Gothic-styled architectural nightmare which was the City Chambers, the centre of Glasgow's municipal administration. The stone's throw distance was apt – the *Bugle* took as poor a view of the efficiency of the city fathers as the fathers did of the *Bugle*'s activities, and a daily barrage of verbal missiles formed a regular trade between the two forces.

Peace apparently reigned, however, as Thane entered the main door of the *Bugle* office and asked at the reception desk for Jock Mills, the paper's crime reporter. The last edition of the day was being run off in a muffled thunder of presses from the basement below, a covey of young messenger boys were playing pontoon with their bus fare money as stakes.

The commissionaire, a thin-faced ex-soldier with a rash of medal ribbons on his tunic, spoke into the internal phone for a moment then called over the nearest of the youngsters. The boy came over, somewhat annoyed at the interruption – with an ace and queen hand, he'd been on the brink of taking over as banker.

'Mr Mills, up in the interview room.' The commission-aire thumbed towards Thane. The boy – sixteen, pimpled, his fingers heavily nicotined – gave a brief nod and led their visitor towards the lift.

'Been here long?' asked Thane.

'Two months.' The youngster pressed the controls and the gates shut.

'Going to be a reporter?' encouraged Thane.

'Me?' The boy was shocked. 'Work round the clock and no overtime? That's for mugs, mister.'

The lift halted before he could detail his own life-plan, and he guided Thane along the door-lined corridor to the interview room, a frosted glass cubicle furnished with a handful of armchairs and an extension phone.

Jock Mills was already there. The *Bugle*'s crime reporter, a cheerful, red-haired young man, greeted him warmly.

'I'll take it this isn't a social call,' he grinned. 'And I haven't trod on anybody's toes lately – so that means you want something.'

Thane looked around him warily. 'This room used to be wired for sound, Jock. You told me about it once, remember?'

The reporter flushed. 'That's only when we want a tape of an interview – some people go pale at the sight of a notebook, you know that. Others have a nasty habit of calling you a liar once their story is in print and they think they can sue.'

Thane accepted it. Jock Mills had built up his police contacts on trust, and that took too long, offered the chance of too many exclusive stories over the average year, to throw away for a one-day sensation.

'What can you tell me about this, Jock?' He took a thick manilla envelope from his pocket and waited while the reporter opened out the folded newspaper it contained – the paper Phil Moss had found in the Ford's glove box.

'Yesterday's – an early edition.' The younger man gave Thane a shrewd glance. 'It's important?'

'Maybe.'

'Something to do with the Shashkov affair?' He chuckled at the Millside chief's stoney-faced reaction. 'We're splashing the Edinburgh bomb attempt – everybody is. But still

107

not one whisper about the four gents from a certain trawler.'

'Which is probably wise,' growled Thane.

'No comment.' The reporter gave a sardonic shake of his head. 'We've been on to the trawlermen angle for days. Our local corr. tipped us off the day after they got ashore, just about the time the fifth man gave himself up. The story was set and ready when the editor was handed a Ministry "D" notice. He didn't fancy a spell in jail, so the story was killed.' Mills shrugged. 'We've a free press, as long as it behaves itself. Anyway, what about this paper?'

'Does the *Bugle* circulate as far north as Aberfeldy?'

'No . . .' Jock Mills turned its pages casually then stopped at the centre spread, a new interest dawning. 'But this edition would go even further north. Mind if I bring the circulation manager in on this? His name's Vaughan – he's all right.'

Thane nodded agreement and waited while Mills used the internal telephone. The *Bugle*'s circulation manager, a portly, bow-tied bustler, joined them within a minute. Once Jock Mills had shown him the paper he displayed the same interest.

'We call this a "slip" edition,' he explained. 'The *Bugle* loses a lot of circulation in the summer and autumn, readers going off on holiday – and to try and hold on to some of it we send the paper after them. These slip editions are identical with our regular issues except for one inside page. We slip a new page in for a limited run, maybe a thousand copies, maybe more, for each of a dozen or so holiday centres . . . you know the sort of thing, happy family groups on the beach, what's on at the local cinema, lucky prizewinners in our promenade competitions.' He grimaced. 'It costs money, the return is small and the page layout is usually a mess. But it keeps the circulation figures looking a little brighter.'

'And this one?'

'Went to Aberdeen.' The circulation manager pointed to the picture page before him. 'Horrible, isn't it?'

'You mean this paper couldn't be bought anywhere else?'

'Definitely no.'

'But some copies would be kept here?'

'One or two.' The man hesitated. 'Then, of course, the delivery driver might hand out a few on the way north.' He fingered his bow tie and gave Thane a sly glance. 'Ever known a police station that didn't have a free supply of papers for the men on office duty? It always helps when one of our boys gets booked for speeding . . .'

Thane made a diplomatic retreat. 'This paper didn't come from a police station. Where else?'

'Level crossing operators get them, cafés where the drivers stop for a meal – look, I'll try and locate the man who did yesterday's Aberdeen run.'

It took a few minutes. The driver concerned was out on a local news-stand round, and they had to wait until he returned to the *Bugle*'s despatch bay for a fresh load. But when Thane left the newspaper office he had a list of half a dozen places where spare copies of the Aberdeen slip edition had been handed out.

The three which mattered most were all in the Fife area. The *Bugle* van had been on a two-stage run, one half of its papers due to be off-loaded at Kirkcaldy, a regular edition delivery point. From there, the special slip edition had travelled north through Fife, crossed the River Tay by vehicle ferry, and then rejoined the main road for Aberdeen. It was far away from the Glen Lyon district, but a route which passed only a double handful of miles distant from both St. Andrews and Sunbury Colliery, General Shashkov's two Saturday stopping places!

He halted at the pavement's edge and glanced at his watch. In just over an hour he was due to see Dan Laurence again. The three places in Fife where the driver had handed over slip editions were a café, a filling station and a shop where he'd stopped to buy cigarettes. The sooner Phil Moss had the addresses and could check them out the better.

Thane said a sad goodbye to his hopes of a meal at home and settled for a telephone at Headquarters and egg and chips in the police canteen.

# Chapter Six

Hunched in the front seat of a Fife county patrol car, Detective Inspector Moss eyed the brightly lit shop across the roadway in jaundiced gloom. Since Thane's telephone message had finally reached him, he'd tracked down two of the three slip edition copies of the *Bugle* – and that apparently simple task had taken him nearly two hours.

On the surface, it had seemed simple enough – certainly better than the job of plodding around questioning the Old Course green-keeping staff. They were used to visiting strangers arriving, treated them as commonplace, and could only shake their heads over the descriptions he kept repeating.

The county car and driver were awaiting him, and he'd left the course right away. This same little general store they were now parked opposite had been the nearest and first on his list, about ten miles from St. Andrews, on the outskirts of Cupar, one of the many small towns in the area. But on the first visit the shop assistant had known nothing about the newspaper and the owner was out on a delivery run and not due back for some time.

He'd moved on. The two other places, the filling station and the café, were both at Glenrothes, another ten miles south. The filling station's copy was easy enough to trace – torn into squares, it was hanging on a nail in the mechanics' wash-room. At the café, he thought he'd struck better fortune when the proprietor remembered giving his copy away. The snag was that half a dozen 'regulars' had been in the place at the time and he couldn't remember which of them had taken it. Moss had found out for him, the hard way, had scored the café off his list – and now the general store represented the last chance.

'Think you'll have better luck here, sir?' His driver, a bulky Fifer with a neat bristling moustache, was beginning to feel equally disgruntled.

'Huh!' Moss glared again at the shop's beacon-like windows. Dusk had faded into darkness on their return trip to the town, and the car's sidelights cast their own dull glow by the kerbside. 'He's probably using the paper to wrap up groceries.' A twinkle of lights a little way along the road caught his eye. 'What's that place?'

'The huts?' The driver relaxed a little behind the wheel. 'Sort of a holiday camp, sir – pre-fab chalets, home-made huts, that sort of thing. Used to be a couple of converted buses too, but the council said that was a bit much, and they had to move on.'

Moss nodded. He'd vaguely noticed the collection on their first visit – the Fife holiday coast and its neighbouring inland had several similar spots.

'Here goes.' He got out of the car and crossed over.

The 'ting' of the shop bell as he opened the door brought a small fat butterball of a man hurrying from the room at the rear. The shopkeeper beamed across the counter, one chubby band resting lightly on a mound of pre-packed cheese.

'Police.' Moss slapped his warrant card on the counter.

'The girl told me you'd been.' The man chuckled. 'She thought it was something to do with a newspaper, but she always gets things tangled.'

'This time she was right,' Moss told him. 'A van driver says he gave you a copy of the Glasgow *Bugle* yesterday, when he stopped off for cigarettes.'

'That's right.' The moon-shaped face reddened a little. 'Why? He's stopped here before, that bloke – always gives me one. Says he usually has a few spares.'

'Nothing wrong with him giving you it,' Moss reassured him. 'What matters is, do you still have it?'

The shopkeeper's fingers rapped a soft, thoughtful tattoo on the cheese. 'Well . . . no.' Like most fat men, when his smile died the expression which remained was almost lugubrious. 'You see, we don't get evening papers around here – not normally, anyway. You've got to go further into town for them. One of the fellows from the huts came in for groceries – sugar and a pound of cooked ham, it was – and he happened to see the paper on the counter. He asked me if he could have it. Surprised me a bit, but I said yes.'

'Surprised you?'

'Well, him being some kind of foreigner.'

'Medium height, sturdy build, grey hair, small moustache – about my age?' Moss reeled off Serviev's description and felt a sudden thrill of tension.

'Younger maybe, but that's him – a decent bloke. They all are.'

'All? You mean there are more of them in one of the huts?'

'Four of them, though he's the only one I've really spoken to at all.' The shopkeeper pulled the loose skin on one cheek. 'I wondered about renting them the hut, but they're a quiet bunch, and there've been no complaints from any of the other families.'

It took another half-dozen questions to squeeze out that the shopkeeper owned three of the huts on the holiday ground and rented them out as a handy extra income. He'd had a vacancy sign hanging three days before, the result of a last-minute cancellation, and the men had arrived out of the blue and taken the booking.

'Ten quid a week, power and television thrown in.' He was worried now. 'They . . . they seemed all right.'

'Did they have a car, a grey Ford?' Moss took the man's nod in his stride. 'And they're still living in the hut?'

113

'Well, they've paid till the end of the week – though I haven't seen the car around tonight.'

'It won't be back,' said Moss dryly. 'Which hut?'

Second chalet on the left in the rear row, the shopkeeper told him – and was still pulling at his cheek as Moss went out. As the door clanged shut, the thin, wiry inspector stopped on the pavement for a moment, looking along at the holiday ground, then made up his mind. He crossed to the waiting car and gave a brief nod as the driver looked out of his opened window.

'We're on to something this time.' He thumbed back over his shoulder. 'I'm going to have a scout round one of those huts – while I'm doing it, call control and ask 'em to stand by for a possible assistance call. If there's anyone at home over there we'll need help before we knock on the door.'

'You said there would only be three of them, sir.' The Fifer stroked his moustache. 'I don't mind a wee bit o' a rough-house.'

'You're more likely to get a stick of gelignite shoved down your throat if these laddies play rough,' growled Moss. 'Get on with it.'

The Fife man winced a little and reached for the microphone, making a mental note that this particular terrier had teeth. Satisfied, Moss tucked his hands deep into the pockets of his flapping dirty-white raincoat and headed for the holiday huts, his pace neither fast nor slow, walking through the entrance with the air of a visitor who knew where he was going but was in no desperate rush to get there.

In all, there were about forty huts in the collection, scattered in rough, unplanned rows. The main pathway was a mixture of rough tarmac and rougher road chips, dimly lit by one meagre line of weak electric bulbs strung between wires. Every few yards, an unlit side path led off to either side. He took the third path to the left, strolling into its darkness, hands still in his pockets. A few of the huts around had lights burning behind their drawn curtains. He heard music coming from one, and the ghostly blue-white flicker of a television screen varied its intensity through another lightly veiled window.

He left the path beside one dark, silent structure which appeared to owe its basic creation to a variety of packing cases and took to the darker shadows, moving quietly, striking towards the rear of the camp area.

There were six huts in the rear row, and the storekeeper's chalet was easily recognizable for two reasons. It bulked the largest, and it was the only one without lights.

Moss eased forward, his footsteps muffled by the soft turf. At the chalet door he stopped, listened, pressed his ear against the wood, still heard nothing, and tried the handle. It turned. With his free hand he drew out the sawn-off lead-loaded, strictly non-regulation baton from his inside pocket. The door creaked a little as he pushed it open, but the house remained still. He waited another long moment then, decision made, fumbled for the light switch and the bulb in the little hallway blazed to life. The baton still at the ready, he began a cautious search.

The chalet was empty, but it hadn't been that way for long. The glowing stove, the smell of tobacco smoke in the air, the greasy dishes piled in the tiny kitchen sink, the still tepid coffee pot, all emphasized the point. The place had been kept reasonably tidy, but then, the men who'd been using it had travelled light – and trawlermen, living in confined space, soon learn the elementary rules of housekeeping.

Moss frowned uneasily. Had Kelch and his two companions taken fright at Serviev's non-return and decided to move on? He stooped beside the stove as a glint of metal caught his eye. Some scraps of sheet tin, a soldering iron and a length of wire solder lay side by side in an old cardboard shoe-box.

There was something wrong, something very wrong –

he sensed it rather than realized anything positive. On a sudden hunch, he crossed to the television set in one corner and laid his hand on the cabinet. It was warm to the touch – only minutes could have passed since it had been in use.

Moss headed for the door. He reached it, switched out the hall light, and stepped into the dark of the night. It took his eyes a brief second to re-adjust, and that was long enough. A vague shape detached itself from the wall at his side and he was still turning, still raising the baton, when the blow fell.

Detective Inspector Moss slumped down, his mind blanking red midway through a half-formed curse at his own stupidity.

Two other men joined his assailant, stepping silently from the shadows. The tallest chuckled, then joined his companions in dragging the unconscious figure back into the chalet.


'Belt them on the skull – that's an old-fashioned philosophy. The trouble with today's average cop is that he doesn't realize that he needs brain, not brawn.' Detective Superintendent Laurence was once again happily mounted on his pet hobbyhorse.

'All right, Dan, I'm not arguing.' Colin Thane gave a sigh and looked hopefully at the pair of shoes on the laboratory table between them. He'd returned to the Scientific Branch exactly on schedule. Dan Laurence had agreed he was ready, but so far was showing no inclination to hurry. 'You said there was something interesting about Serviev's shoes . . .'

'Uh? Oh, aye – aye, that's right.' Laurence blew his nose loudly on a khaki army-surplus handkerchief then lifted the footwear. 'Well, for a start we found the odd fleck o' grass an' grass seed on them. Then there was some sand engrained around the soles and in the welt o' the uppers.

116

The sand had a trace or two o' bone meal, Colin – and the microscope showed one or two grains o' the same combination around the tip o' yon wee golf tee you brought in. Which leads me to the inspired deduction that he'd been walking, probably playing, over a seaside golf course . . . it was shore sand, not inland stuff, and bone meal's a regular top dressing for many a golf course.' He held the shoes closer to the light, satisfaction in his eyes. 'But we're no' finished. Take a look at the leather at the toes. See how it's pretty badly scuffed?'

Thane rubbed his thumb lightly over the leather, feeling the rough scoring which marred its surface. 'What about it?'

'It's good and bad.' Laurence shook his head. 'Sorry, Colin, I know you're thinking about Shashkov's game o' golf tomorrow. But you'd maybe better keep an open mind. We got fragments o' coal and sandstone grit out o' these cuts, and more o' both from his clothes and shoes.'

'Which came first?' Tight-lipped, Thane saw his hopes tangle and crash.

'Well . . .' The Scientific Branch chief frowned and absent-mindedly lit a cigarette. 'On the shoes, the coal grit and sandstone covered the sand and bone meal traces here an' there, so if I had to plump for a choice I'd say he'd been prowlin' around a colliery or a coal-yard o' some kind after he'd been at the golf.' He put down the shoes and sat on the table, legs dangling. 'Another thing, you wouldn't take a rope with you if you were having a game o' golf, would you? Yet we found a whole lot o' wee rope fibres on his clothes.'

'Why take a rope to a colliery?'

'Hell, how should I know?' protested Laurence. 'But he's been rubbin' against rope, Colin – and by the amount o' fibres we found, it was no casual contact.'

On what facts they had, Dan Laurence had made the only choice he could. Perhaps Kelch and his comrades had examined the Old Course then rejected it as posing too many problems, turned their attention instead to Sunbury Colliery, the next stop on Shashkov's Saturday programme.

The rope – it could mean anything or nothing. It could be an ingredient in Kelch's next move – for the moment, Thane tucked it aside in his mind.

'Anything else, Dan?'

'Nothing that matters – not yet, anyway.' The Scientific Branch chief nodded his shaggy head towards the next bench, where two of his 'lads' were at work. 'We're having a wee look at what came down from the crashed Ford, but so far there's been nothing spectacular.'

Thane glanced at his watch. 'Then I'd better move. Buddha Ilford should be back by now, and you can guess what he's going to ask.'

'Well, it won't be the state of the weather,' nodded Laurence wryly. 'The best of British luck, friend – you'll need it.'

It was a mild, starlit night outside, but the chill in Chief Superintendent Ilford's office had no connection with the weather. He waved Thane to the chair opposite, lit his pipe with slow, deliberate care, and took a few puffs in absolute silence.

'I've been out for the last two hours. Any idea why?'

'The duty man said you'd got a line on a bank embezzlement,' said Thane cautiously.

'That's one side of the coin.' Ilford set down his pipe in the big ashtray beside him. 'The other is I wanted to hide from this ruddy telephone. You know why?' He gave a rumbling bark. 'Because since noon today it's been ringing non-stop, one dam' fool official after another, right up the ladder – everyone but the ruddy Prime Minister, all wanting to know why we haven't nailed Kelch and his pals. "Do we realize how serious it all is?"' He mimicked officialdom in a vicious, squeaking parody, then scowled. 'All right, now it's my turn, Colin. What the hell's happening – or when is it going to? Do I have to wait for the newspapers?'

Thane met the city C.I.D. chief's glare and felt his own temper rise. 'We're trying – you know that,' he replied stubbornly. 'We got Serviev this afternoon, Phil Moss is checking another lead right now, the Scientific Branch and plenty others have been working their guts out. . . .' In the same deliberate, coldly factual voice he catalogued the situation through every detail. 'That's how it stands, sir. Unless' – the ice in his manner matched Ilford's – 'unless, of course, you've any fresh approach in mind.'

A slow, twitching grin began in one corner of Buddha Ilford's mouth and spread. 'All right, we've snarled at each other. Let's leave it. If it helps, one bright Whitehall type suggested we should have a Scotland Yard team flown north. I told him we were already co-operating to the full with Home Office security, that Scotland Yard, whether he knew it or not, was a purely English firm and had no powers in Scotland, that we'd never needed their help in my lifetime and that we didn't propose to start now.'

He struck another match for his pipe, watched Thane over the flame, and mused half to himself. 'A few flecks of coal dust aren't sufficient on their own to satisfy me the next try will be at the colliery.'

'They could easily have given both places a looking over before they made any decision,' agreed Thane. Inwardly, he was indignant. Had Buddha imagined he was going to thump all his eggs in one basket? 'I'd grant that the odds might have swayed a fraction against the Old Course, sir – but nothing more.'

Satisfied, Ilford thumbed through the memos on his desk until he found the one he wanted. 'Probably academic now, but the Army came through with Herrald's service record. Called up in 1941, commissioned in the Royal Engineers in '42, wounded and transferred to the Royal Army Service Corps in '44, demobbed as a captain. No decorations, no black marks. As for this story of Lady

Dunspar's that he suggested he could smuggle Kelch and his friends out of the country, there's a strong chance he could have done it. I put a couple of men on checking round some of his business contacts.'

'They confirmed?'

'They did more than that. Herrald has – or maybe had – some pretty good connections in the shipping business thanks to his import-export trading. A couple of them admitted he telephoned them last Friday evening, wanting to know sailing dates on the Atlantic run and hinting he might be trying for a rather special favour.' Ilford stopped as the telephone at his side gave a double ring. He looked at the instrument with something close to loathing then, as it rang again, sighed and answered.

'Ilford here . . .' As the C.I.D. chief spoke, Thane began to relax back in his chair then leaned forward again at Buddha's next words. 'Yes, he's with me. What's happening at your end?'

The voice at the other end of the line spoke for almost a minute. Ilford grunted from time to time, his face gradually changing from interest through disbelief to despair. At last, he gave a groan. 'All right – tell him yourself.' He practically threw the receiver across the desk-top. 'It's Moss. He's not only lost them, he's gone and lost his ruddy car into the bargain!'

Thane took over the call. 'Phil?'

'I heard him.' Phil Moss's voice came sad and wearily over the line. 'I'll keep it brief, Colin. The newspaper angle paid off. They were living in a hut in a holiday camp outside Cupar, and I went to have a look. But they must have been edgy because of Serviev – probably had somebody keeping an eye on the camp gate. The hut was empty when I went in, but when I came out somebody belted me on the skull.'

Thane could do little more than commiserate with the rest of Moss's tale. When he'd come round, he'd been lying in the chalet and his raincoat was missing. He'd staggered back to the main gate, and tripped over the county police driver lying unconscious between two of the huts.

Finding their car had been taken completed Moss's burden of humiliation. When the driver came round, all he could tell was that he'd seen someone whom he'd taken to be Moss, somebody wearing the same dirty-white raincoat, beckoning to him from the camp gate. He'd got out of the car and sprinted over – while the figure in the raincoat moved back inside the camp, waiting beside a darkened hut. Then someone had stepped out behind him and he too had been thumped on the head.

'Any trace of the car yet, Phil?'

'None,' said Moss unhappily. 'There's a radio alert out for it, which should have made interesting listening. And some of the county blokes are here now. How's Buddha?'

Thane flickered a glance across the desk. 'The forecast mentioned a deep depression – possible storms. Stay put, Phil. I'll be up as soon as I can.'

'Right.' He heard his second-in-command sigh and then the click as the faraway telephone was replaced.

Buddha Ilford had a suspicious frown on his broad, normally placid face as Thane turned towards him. 'What was that about storms?' he demanded.

'It looks like being another all-night session up there,' said Thane easily. 'Phil wanted to know what the weather would be like.'

Ilford gave a snort of only part belief. 'Well, you'd better get moving. I'll contact Colonel Donnan and bring him up-to-date . . . which will be another happy little interlude. When you see Moss, tell him . . . tell him . . . no, leave it. That's going to be my pleasure.' He struck another match for his pipe, scraped the wood too savagely, and cursed as the blazing match head snapped and landed in his correspondence tray. Tamping out the potential bonfire, he totally ignored Thane's departure.

*     *     *

121

The Headquarters driver had eaten, rested, and was in fine fettle for the journey north. The Jaguar sang its way over the long, quiet miles of road and it was barely ten p.m. by a church clock as it slowed to a purring crawl through the streets of Cupar and finally halted at the holiday ground.

'Get it over with,' begged Moss, coming forward from the camp entrance as Thane left the car. 'What did Buddha say, Colin?'

'He's saving it for later.' Thane fell into step with him. 'Found your car yet?'

'No.' Moss kicked a loose stone ahead of him. 'They've probably dumped it by now and acquired something different.'

'How's the head?'

'Sore – in more ways than one.' His thin face was bitter in the dull glow from the wire-strung path lights. 'I feel a ruddy idiot. How were things in Glasgow?'

Thane told him as they neared the chalet door.

Moss gave a sad shake of his head as the Millside chief finished. 'Well, I can't add much. I've talked with people in the other huts, and had another session with the store-keeper. They're vague on descriptions, only certain that four men were here and that the Ford was parked outside. They left early in the morning and weren't usually back till late evening.' Moss nodded to the uniformed constable on duty outside the chalet and waved his companion on. 'Welcome to Kelch's Castle,' he punned viciously. 'After tonight, the county boys will probably rename it Moss's Misery.'

They went in through the little hallway to the main room, where two Fife C.I.D. men were already in occupancy.

'We've done the usual, sir,' said the older of the two as Moss finished the introductions. 'Plenty of dabs all over the place, but we've still to sort 'em out.'

'They're not worrying about leaving traces.' Thane

glanced towards the two doors leading from the room. 'What's behind those?'

'Bedrooms,' contributed Moss. 'Left a couple of dirty shirts behind in one, a few bits and pieces in the other. Here's the collection.' He crossed over to the sideboard close by the stove. The results of the search were piled on its top . . . a comb and a handkerchief, a half-used tube of toothpaste, all the other minor, anonymous items which men might overlook or abandon when they prepared to quit in a hurry.

Thane raked through the heap with scant enthusiasm. 'That's the lot?'

'Apart from a few magazines and this soldering kit.' Phil Moss lifted the cardboard box from its place beside the stove and dumped it in front of Thane. 'Looks as if they've been passing the time by building another little surprise package.'

'Uh-huh.' The scraps of tinplate, rough-cut by metal shears, were assorted in shape and size. One or two bore traces of pencilled lines where shears had cut slightly off their marked path. Thane pieced a few together and whistled gently through his teeth as he examined the result. 'Not much help, are they? Could be trimmings from a box, a canister, any dam' thing.'

'And guaranteed nasty and clever.' Moss ran one hand tenderly over the top of his head.

Thane moved over to the stove, lifted its lid, glanced in at the glowing coals, then closed it again and nodded to the county men. 'Better have this fire extinguished and the ashes fine-riddled . . .'

'Clever to a point, Phil, but that's all they've been so far. A revolver shot at long range – that's the idea of an optimistic amateur. The pillar-box bomb was different, but to be any way sure of the result they'd have needed a hell of a sight more explosives than they could get through that letter slot in one small package.'

'They're trying hard, give them that much.' Moss

scowled, went over to the sink, ran some water from the tap into a glass, and used it to wash down a pill. 'Agh. Well, what next?'

Thane eyed him closely. Phil Moss's normal pallor was intensified by the lines of strain around his eyes, the tight set of his lips. 'You look as though you could use something stronger than tap-juice, Phil. And some food, decent food. After that, we move over to St. Andrews – nice and handy to welcome Donnan when he brings up Shashkov and company in the morning. We'll base ourselves in the local cop shop, have them lay on two telephones, and then we start dredging. Every village cop, every garage, every pub we can wake to life. . . . Kelch hasn't been wasting his time. He's pretty certainly been having a good look around, doing his homework so that nothing is left to chance. Where he's been and when, that's what we've got to find out.'

They were high and dry, stranded, with little more than ten hours to go before Shashkov's visit to Fife got under way. Stranded, without any real lead to follow and left with only the angry helplessness, the gnawing frustration of having found yet another trail only to once more have it peter out to nothing.

Thane looked again at the little fragments of scrapped tinplate, fragments which held a secret of their own. Another radio-controlled bomb? Donnan had promised he'd organize some form of jamming device. But Martin Kelch was unlikely to try the same idea twice, and a shop-to-shop dragnet still hadn't been able to trace the sale of the first, let alone a second, radio-controlled set in the period since the trawlermen had landed. He shrugged and brushed the tinplate fragments back into a heap.

'Come on . . . food.'


By eleven-fifteen they'd eaten, were installed in St. Andrews police station, and the operators at the local

124

telephone exchange were handling the first of the torrent of calls ahead. At eleven-forty, the missing police car was found abandoned in a lane near the village of Kennoway, eight miles from where it had been stolen. Ten minutes later, the police office at Kennoway was back on the line again. A local vet, preparing to answer an emergency call from one of the farms around, had discovered that his blue Wolseley 1500 saloon had been whisked away from the garage behind his house.

By midnight, Moss knew his switchboard operator's first name was Maisie and that she worked nights because her fiancé was a merchant seaman. On the practical side, he'd located the owner of a village pub a mile or so from Sunbury Colliery. The man had a vague recollection of two strangers being in his bar at noon two days before, and thought they'd driven off in a grey car. Tourists, he'd guessed from their accents. Descriptions? No, he couldn't remember what they'd been like.

To balance, Thane had an indignant St. Andrews garage man whom he had roused from sleep. He'd filled the tank of a grey Ford Zephyr the previous day, one man aboard it. But he'd been too busy to do more than work the pump and take the money, and the customer was only the vaguest of memories.

Outside the warmth of the station, the same quest was occupying the energies of a considerable section of the strength of three county forces around them; mobile units searching for the blue Wolseley, village cops dragged from their beds to their bicycles in a prowling search for strangers, town beatmen checking hotels and vacant buildings, camp sites and bed-and-breakfast bungalows. Two squads had more specific tasks – one to guard the entrances to Sunbury Colliery, the other to patrol in pairs the sprawling expanse of the Old Course.

Thirty minutes after Saturday had begun, Dan Laurence telephoned through from Glasgow, spent considerable wrath describing how every blanking telephone line into

125

St. Andrews police station seemed to have been engaged for the last few blanking hours, then finally came round to the reason for his call.

'If you're still interested, here's what we've got from the crashed Ford,' he rumbled. 'Underwing and tyre examination show only shore sand and road grit, no traces of coal or sandstone. But the grit we vacuumed up from the ear floor had one or two flakes o' coal among it, the same sandstone grains and rope fibre. That's from both back and front seats, Colin.'

An aimless doodle spread across Thane's pad of scrap-paper as he listened. A little man and a big bomb, both surrounded by what could have been a floral wreath. One day he'd save some of these doodles and thump them down in front of a psychiatrist. No, maybe he wouldn't. The findings might be too close for comfort. He tapped the ballpoint for a moment.

'Colin?' The Scientific Branch chief's voice came grumphing over the wire.

'Still here, Dan.' He drew a golf ball, then added a smouldering fuse. 'You found sand in his shoes –'

'And on the car floor,' confirmed Laurence. 'The odd bit o' grass and a speck or two o' bone meal as well. Finger-prints are pretty much as you'd expect – one set identified as Serviev's, three others matching the ones tabbed "unknown" from the cottage.'

Coal and grass, the colliery or the Old Course – the same puzzle as before. More and more Thane's instincts pulled against the first possibility, despite the evidence of the dust layers.

There was that hint of the spectacular in setting the next attempt on Shashkov's life at the Old Course, before a massed audience. It was a touch more in keeping with what he'd learned of Kelch's character than a killing amid the grime of a colliery.

'Any more word from Professor MacMaster, Dan?' He asked more from habit than hope.

'Aye, he looked in about an hour back,' said Laurence. 'He'd heard you'd been around Headquarters – wanted to tell you something about the mould on those food tins he collected from the cottage. Called it an "interesting phenomenon".' The Scientific Branch chief gave a sardonic chuckle. 'Anyway, you'll see him in the morning. He's driving up to St. Andrews – for a week-end rest, according to him. You know what that means. If anyone gets killed, the bald-headed old buzzard wants to be nice and near.'

They said goodbye and Thane hung up. The station sergeant had been brewing tea, and the taste of that strong, almost scalding liquid had seldom been sweeter. He looked over the top of the mug towards Phil Moss and mustered a grin. 'It could be worse, I suppose. At least we don't have to foot the phone bill.' He lit a cigarette, and left the packet on the desk.

His second-in-command watched for a moment, then crossed over and silently helped himself to one.

'Thought you'd stopped.' Thane tossed him the matches.

'——' The word wasn't usually heard outside of Glasgow, but it was superbly tailored to fit the feelings of one tired, soreheaded, particularly miserable detective inspector.

They had their first break an hour later, and almost simultaneously a surprise visitor. The break was a radio message from one of the mobile units. The stolen Wolseley had been found abandoned, half-hidden under a railway culvert two miles from St. Andrews. Unless the little group of men they hunted were trying a final bluff – Thane's craggy face hardened. No, if there was any bluff intended it was a double measure, the kind dreamed up by a mind which could expect the police to ponder beyond the obvious and which was prepared to exploit that very possibility. The other facet, of course, was that Kelch might feel his plans were now so well laid that nothing could go wrong.

127

The visitor was Colonel Donnan, a weary-eyed, blue-stubbled figure who gulped a mug of tea then peeled off his coat and slumped into a chair. 'After Ilford told me what was happening I thought I'd better gallop up and join you,' he told them. 'Anything more I should know?'

Thane talked and the little Irishman listened, nursing a cigarette. When Thane had finished, Donnan looked away from him for a moment, staring at the plain, cream-painted wall, gnawing gently on his lip. Then he nodded. 'The golf course it is – and there's no sense trying to persuade Shashkov to cancel the game. I've tried. But the publicity he's been getting is doing just what we guessed – making him a hero back home. He's loving it.' He reached for the telephone. 'Well, I didn't want to do this, but I've no option. Whether we look dam' fools or not, there'll be no public gallery following him around – and anyone found on the Old Course while he's there lands in a cell until it's over.' As the operator answered, he placed a priority call to Army Scottish Command in Edinburgh then, hand over the mouthpiece, made his own weary comment. 'Why couldn't he have stuck to chess, like all the rest of his mob?'

The call came through and he got busy. But it was already too late. Fate's carefully constructed rendezvous was out there in the darkness, positioned and ready just as it had been since an hour before midnight.

# Chapter Seven

When the sun shines, the Old Course at St. Andrews, readily acknowledged the most famous and oldest golf course in the world, lays claim to a third title – the most beautiful. Starting as a narrow neck of flawless green turf, fringed on one side by the grey-blue waters of the North Sea, on the other by the tall, calm, stone-built dignity of the university town, it broadens beyond into a plump, tempting expanse of rolling fairways which are ridged and bounded by whin and gorse, their greens unique in their cunning, baize-smooth hills and valleys.

Plump, tempting – and deadly, as even the most experienced practitioner of the art of club-swinging has discovered to his shaken cost. To play the Old Course is a love-hate ordeal which begins from the very moment the player stands on what has been called the loneliest spot in the world, the first tee. Ahead lies his challenge and his first obstacle, the shallow, gentle-flowing Swilken Burn. To one side, the austere clubhouse of the Royal and Ancient Golf Club seems to sneer at his bravado in coming here. Behind, deadliest of all, wait the constant, silently critical audience of golfing addicts whose cold appraisal knows neither warmth nor kindness. At the first tee, even steel-nerved low-handicap men have swung, missed the ball, and carved chunks from the sacred turf in their moment of nervous tension.

Out beyond, where the gorse flaunts its flanking threats, another danger lies hidden – the yawning, trap-mouthed sand bunkers with menace in their very names. The Beardies and Coffins, Nick's and the Pulpit, Hell and the Grave, Cat's Trap and Lion's Mouth, Principal's Nose and the Wig are constant and ready.

The Old Course, in short, is a disease. A fatal, irresistible infection 6,545 yards long with a standard scratch score of 73 and a casualty rate measured in husbandless wives and fat, happy traders who sell golf balls, tees, aspirins, instruction books and similar aids.

That it was closed to play for the morning had been publicized before – with a fresh reminder in the screaming headlines with which every morning paper in the country followed up the Shashkov bomb attempt story and spun webs of conjecture round the security precautions to be taken during the Communist leader's visit to St. Andrews.

But sportsmen usually start at the back of their newspaper and seldom reach page one's contents. Before breakfast the first straggling club-laden arrivals had already been turned away by the police patrols on duty around the starter's box.

At 9.30 a.m., a cold-edged wind blowing in from the sea despite the cloudless sky, the young policeman on duty at the main entrance shivered a little as he tried to ram the point home.

'Sorry, Dad, but it's final. You'll have to wait till afternoon if you want a game.' He grinned sympathetically. 'Look, why not go and get yourself a nice cup o' coffee, eh?'

'Blast your coffee and I'm not your father!' Mr William Wallace, a stout, elderly figure in an old Norfolk jacket, antiquated plus-fours and tweed cap, his much repaired pencil golf bag and its collection of wooden-shafted clubs slung over one shoulder, was becoming angry. It showed in the violent red hue gathering over his face, in the way his false teeth clicked to emphasize each word. 'I'm a ratepayer of this town, I know my rights, and no fluffy-faced young – young dressed-up schoolboy is going to rob me of them!'

The constable flushed. He only needed a quick mow with an electric razor once a week, but . . . 'Now listen, Dad –'

'You listen!' William Wallace stormed on with all the valour of the Scottish hero whose name he bore. 'Every Saturday morning for the last forty-six years I've had my round over the Old Course. Every Saturday, bar the time I got married and had to go away for the honeymoon! This is a public course, isn't it?'

'Yes, but –'

'And any citizen of St. Andrews has the right to use it, provided he's paid his green fees? Isn't there a parchment covenant which guarantees it?'

'I know, Dad. Signed in 1552 – we had it thumped into us at school.' The youngster tried another tack. 'But there've been other Saturdays like this now and again, haven't there? Say the Open Championship is on, you don't expect to go bashing your way out through the field, do you? Or if the course is closed because of the weather –'

'There isn't a championship and the weather's fine.' William Wallace glared around at the bustle of blue and khaki uniforms around. 'There's just a damned awful fuss about some Bolshevik who'd more likely been thrown in jail in my young days.' He gave a final, angry clack of his teeth. 'Now, do I get my rights or not?'

The youngster shook his head. 'Sorry, not till the afternoon.'

A sergeant and another constable were ambling towards them, attracted by the row. William Wallace jerked his golf bag higher on his shoulder with a defiant rattle of clubs, gave a loud sniff in the direction of the reinforcements, and stumped off. If they thought they'd heard the last of this – he scowled again, then headed for the nearest coffee shop.

131

Behind him, the uniformed men exchanged grins. The sergeant sucked a peppermint, glanced at his watch, then murmured a warning as he spotted the quartet walking along the shore road towards them.

A shave, a fresh shirt and a good breakfast had refuelled Colin Thane's energies. Colonel Donnan was by his side, Phil Moss a pace or two behind with the local police superintendent, who was arrayed in his best uniform complete with neck-rubbing stiff white collar.

'All quiet, sergeant?' The superintendent swept the scene, his worries evident in the only half-attentive way he returned the sergeant's snapped salute.

'So far, sir. All uniformed men in position.'

'Fine – fine.' The superintendent turned to Thane and the others. 'Time I had a last word with the Club people. Any of you want to come along?'

They shook their heads.

'Well now . . .' Colonel Donnan watched the super-intendent stride off, and drew in deep lungfuls of sea-spiced air. 'Half an hour till Shashkov arrives. Any last-minute bright ideas?' His expression was grim as he rested his hands on the painted wooden railing which was the course's boundary. 'Or do we just stand here and wait for it to happen?'

A steady, nearing throb of rotor blades pulled the two C.I.D. men's attention skywards. The big R.A.F. helicopter, its body silver, nose and rotor blades yellow, was coming in over the course about fifty feet up. The nose dipped a fraction, it hovered, then, as the rotor beat changed, it began to move away again, gaining height.

'There's another one around somewhere.' Donnan pursed his lips.

'Over there, out to sea.' Thane spotted the second approaching speck. 'How'll you communicate?'

'Direct walkie-talkie link.'

Donnan had marshalled his resources with care. Colin Thane ran through the details again – details the little

Irishman had finally formulated only a short time before dawn.

The helicopter patrol was only a beginning. The Old Course perimeter was now under the guard of police, a full infantry company from the Black Watch and an R.A.F. Regiment dog-handling squad. Within their cordon other R.A.F. guard dogs and their handlers were already covering the gorsed and bunkered grassland in regular search patterns.

Another, equally purposeful, sweep had already been completed. At dawn, two truckloads of Royal Engineers had arrived, unloaded their sensitive mine-detector gear, and had launched a slow, steady search of the tees, main paths, greens, all the other places where a bomb might have been planted. While they'd worked, a smaller team had been busy in the clubhouse, setting up a compact but powerful transmitter jamming unit which they guaranteed would block any attempt to repeat the radio-controlled bang of the previous day.

And for the game itself, while the two helicopters prowled overhead, Donnan's final force would operate – thirty picked Special Branch and W.D. security men operating as a screen around and ahead of the two golfers.

Thane pulled his cigarettes from his pocket, found three left, handed them round, then tossed the crumpled, empty packet into a litter bin. 'You've done your share, Donnan. It seems watertight.' He shrugged. 'I wish I could say the same, but what's left for us to chew on?'

'Nothing.' Phil Moss sourly beat the security man to a reply. 'Absolutely nothing – you know it.' There were police still on their routine of search throughout the town, others on roadblocks on the routes leading into it, but beyond that their entire investigation seemed to have come to a grinding halt.

'There's always this report old MacMaster's bringing up, but it sounds pretty useless.' Thane shook his head in a dull stubbornness. 'Yet I've a feeling about it all – a feeling we've had a chance somewhere and missed it. If we'd had more time . . .'

But they hadn't. Buddha Ilford had hammered around that same theme when Thane had spoken to him by telephone before breakfast. Outside of that, the city C.I.D. chief had passed on the only cheering piece of information of the day – the police motor cyclist injured in the Edinburgh bomb blast was improving, should recover all right.

The minutes passed. They smoked, talked a little, and Donnan went off once for a brief discussion with two of his men. When he returned, the local sergeant conjured up some paper cups filled with lukewarm tea. Gradually the grass bank on the opposite side of the road from the course began filling as a crowd gathered, held well back by a line of blue-uniformed police and khaki-clad army men.

The cavalcade bringing the Soviet Minister for Industrial Development arrived exactly on schedule – five large black cars, the first and last filled with security men. Two of the other three vehicles contained a covey of the Russian's broad-shouldered, dark-suited personal entourage and a handful of accredited pressmen. In the middle car, its CD plates gleaming, Shashkov sat with his golf partner, a portly senior Treasury Minister from London who'd been chosen for the occasion by reason of his indifferent game and professional charm.

'Our boy seems happy enough,' muttered Moss, as Shashkov bounced from his car, already dressed for action in a violent green windcheater, beige slacks and white shoes, a beige cap rammed squarely on his heavy, close-shaven head.

'Glad somebody is.' Thane watched their V.I.P. charge wave a greeting to the crowd and appear unabashed by the cold, dour silence. They were spectators, most of them, nothing more, along to see Shashkov in the same spirit they might have viewed a circus parade – or a funeral. Over to the left, two bearded students unfurled a Ban the

Bomb banner and were promptly submerged as plain-clothes men closed in.

Now the golf bags were produced from the cars. Shashkov's, brand new and complete with matched irons and an orange umbrella, came first and was taken charge of by the veteran Old Course caddy who'd been allocated to the job. The Treasury Minister's bag was smaller, in leather, with little hand-knitted woollen caps covering each club-head.

Other golf bags, equally bulky, were being dragged out. Thane's expression became a wintery smile. He knew their contents, repeater shotguns and light automatic carbines, all the rest of the arsenal of items which would accompany the twosome on their eighteen-hole sporting amble.

'Aye, it's funny, sir.' The county sergeant misread Thane's smile as Shashkov disappeared into the clubhouse. 'From the look of him, he'd be better at howkin' up coal wi' thon clubs than hittin' a poor wee ball.'

'If you'd a coal mine handy.' Thane said it idly. 'Well, he'll see a mine this afternoon – if he gets there in one piece.' He'd just spotted Professor MacMaster trying to find a way through the cordon opposite and having an argument with a burly infantryman in the process.

'We've got coal all right.' The sergeant chuckled. 'But no' in a mine, sir – more like in a bottle, you might say. There's a coal seam along at the rocks by the old castle.'

Thane took a half-step forward, ready to go to Mac-Master's aid, then stopped where he was as the county man's words sank home. 'What do you mean, in a bottle?'

The sudden snap in the detective's voice took the other man by surprise and jerked both Moss and Donnan's attention towards them.

'It's – well, it's just the local name for the dungeon at the castle, sir,' said the sergeant, embarrassed at being the centre of so much interest. 'We call it the bottle dungeon –

135

it's carved out o' the rock in the shape o' one. That's where you'll find the coal seam.'

'Has it been checked?' Thane glanced at Phil Moss and saw swift realization dawning. Taras Serviev had died with a taunting laugh on his lips, a laugh at Thane saying he'd 'worry' about the bottle he was trying to hold to the trapped man's lips. And the toes of Serviev's shoes had been scuffed and scraped by contact with rock and coal – rock and coal which, till that moment, Thane had automatically linked with the colliery next on General Shashkov's programme of visits. If Serviev had found a last, twisted joke in the bottle thrust before him . . . 'Well, what about it? Has the castle been checked?'

'No.' The sergeant bit his lip. 'At least, I don't think so, sir. It's closed up just now – one o' the inside walls is dangerous, and they've stopped visitors going through on tours until it's been repaired a bit.'

They'd seen the castle – it was hard to be in St. Andrews for any length of time without catching a glimpse of the old stronghold. On the shore road, but at the opposite end of the town from the golf course, it was a massive, ruined, roofless stone shell surrounded by a high metal fence. To the rear, what was left of its gaunt fortress walls perched on the edge of a drop of close on a hundred feet of jagged rock to the sea below. Once, it had been an imposing structure. Now, it was one of the many, widely scattered ancient monuments maintained by the Ministry of Works.

'But . . .' Donnan's mouth opened and closed again.

For once, Thane ignored the little Irishman. 'Where do we find the keys to the place, sergeant?'

'The caretaker, sir – he lives fairly near.'

There was a fresh rustle of interest from the crowd in the background. General Shashkov and his partner had re-emerged from the clubhouse and were walking in business-like fashion towards the first tee.

'Let's go and get them.' Thane saw MacMaster still

struggling to reach their party, but the professor would have to wait. 'Phil, you'd better come along too – we'll let you know what happens, Colonel.' He hustled Moss and the sergeant over to the nearest of the waiting police cars, the sergeant gave directions to the startled driver, and the car roared on its way.

The caretaker was at home, listening to the radio. As soon as he'd pulled on his shoes, produced his keys and joined them in the car they were off again, tyres screaming as they rounded a corner and took one of the narrow streets leading back to the shore.

'When did you inspect the place last?' demanded Thane.

The caretaker gripped the seat edge as the car swayed round the last bend. 'Not since Monday – I was told once a week would do until the builders were ready to start.'

The rest of the journey took only a couple of minutes. As the car pulled up outside the locked entrance gate, the castle's skeleton shape silent and apparently empty of life, Thane glanced back for a moment in the direction of the Old Course. Shashkov's game would be under way by now – and with it Colonel Donnan's personal ordeal. Then he was out of the car, standing with the others while the caretaker used the largest of his bunch of keys and swung open the gate.

'Colin,' Phil Moss tapped the lock with his fist, 'this wouldn't take much work to open. A bent nail would practically do the job.'

Thane nodded. 'Any other ways in?'

'Well, yes – there's a path down to the shore.' The caretaker frowned unhappily. 'Look, Chief Inspector, don't blame me if somebody's got in here – the fence is only meant to keep youngsters an' drunks out. There's nothing worth thieving and nobody's going to try to flog the ruddy castle, are they?'

'Forget it.' Thane led the way along the narrow pathway laid out across the grass of the filled-in moat, Moss, the sergeant and the caretaker following at his heels. A thin gust of wind stirred the dust underfoot as they went through the broad, gloomy arch of the castle's main entrance and into the open space beyond, laid out as a grass lawn with benches for visitors and flanked all around by the broken remnants of the great, thick walls which had first been begun over seven hundred years before, to stand through war and siege and bombardment then gradually crumble in the face of time.

'The bottle dungeon's over there . . .' The caretaker pointed to a low stone structure guarded by a heavy door over in the far left corner of the courtyard and selected another key from his jingling ring as they crossed in its direction.

They were two-thirds of the way across when the door ahead suddenly swung open and a figure dived out, heading for the opposite wall. At the same moment, a hoarse, muffled shout reached their ears.

'Look out for more – I'll take him!' Thane barked the warning as he charged to cut off the runaway.

The man ahead, small, slim, his grey raincoat flapping as he ran, realized a moment later that he wouldn't make his goal, a low, almost levelled part of the outer wall leading to a rough scramble down the cliffs below. He hesitated then spun on his heel and headed for a short flight of worn stairs leading to a higher platform. His right hand darted into a pocket of the coat and there was a knife clasped tight in it as he reached the top.

Thane didn't slow. His feet clattered on the stone slabs as he bounded towards the man above who had stopped and now stood panting, that right arm with the knife held far out from his side, its blade bright and waiting. As the burly Millside man's rush carried him on to the platform, the knife arm slashed and even as he twisted to avoid the steel Thane felt a rake of pain across his shoulder.

The knife arm swung back for another wild stroke, but this time Thane was under it. Forefinger rigid, his right hand slammed out towards the man's throat . . . slightly off balance, he missed the nerve centre he'd aimed for but the blow still sent the other man reeling, the knife waving ineffectually, the runaway dazed by the unarmed combat tactic Thane had first learned in a dockside brawl.

He gathered himself for a final pounce, just as the runaway made another desperate scramble, pulling himself from the platform on to a higher portion of wall. Thane grabbed the man's left foot with both hands, twisted, then let go and threw himself back as the knife flashed towards him, thrown with all the strength his opponent possessed. The knife missed, clattering on the platform at his feet – but the effort of the throw cost the climber his grip on the worn stone blocks. He clawed wildly, trying to pull himself upwards, then as Thane came on again he tried to twist his body out of the detective's reach. He failed. Instead, he tumbled from his perch, skidding down the opposite side of the stonework then falling backwards.

The man didn't fall far – less than fifteen feet. But the railings were below, the railings with their long, blunt spikes.

Thane felt the man's scream hit him like a blow to the stomach. He looked down, then turned quickly away, the pain in his shoulder burning again, the long slash through the cloth of his jacket and the shirt below red and sticky with blood.

'Colin . . .' Phil Moss panted up the stairway to his side and winced as he saw the wound. 'Hell, he meant business.'

'Aye.' Thane picked up the knife. It was a twin to the thin, razor-edged fish-gutting knife they'd found in Serviev's car after the crash. 'Damn the things.'

'There's somebody down that dungeon.' Moss looked around, his face grim. 'I thought he could keep for a moment – the caretaker's standing by.'

From below, they heard a shout. The county sergeant, joined by the driver from the police car, had reached the

139

railings and their grotesquely draped burden. His voice was strained as he hailed them again.

'He's still alive, but only just – we canna lift him clear on our own, though. He's unconscious.'

'Don't try it,' Thane shouted back. 'Get what help you need, and a doctor. One of you stay and try to ease him.' If the man below had any chance, it depended on the right care, skilled care, being there as he was lifted clear.

The sergeant nodded, had a quick consultation with his companion, then trotted off at a ponderous run.

'What about you?' Phil Moss eyed Thane anxiously.

'I'll hold together.' Thane knew he'd been lucky. The thickness of his jacket cloth had taken the worst of the knife slash. He explored the wound with his other hand. The cut seemed to run for about six inches, but the bleeding was too regular, the pain when he moved sufficiently subdued for any real damage to have been caused. 'Let's get over to this dam' dungeon.'

'Right.' Moss followed him down the stone stairway. 'Which one was he?' He nodded in the direction of the hidden railings.

'From what I saw of him, Arkan Bretsun – the description matches, small, slim, dark-haired.' Two down now, two to go, and if they were lucky . . . he increased his pace across the centre courtyard to where the caretaker was standing nervously at the entrance to the dungeon doorway. The caretaker's face was white with shock as he stood back to let them enter.

'Watch the roof, sir. . . .' The warning came just as Thane hit his head on the low stone archway. The Millside man cursed, staggered blindly for a step or two, then halted, hardly believing what he saw.

The caretaker had already switched on the electric lights which a thoughtful Ministry of Works had installed so that visitors could savour the horrors of the little room in maximum comfort. It was a small, windowless cell with a vaulted roof, the middle of the floor a dark hole rimmed by a waist-high wall.

'Down there?' Thane's voice echoed the disbelief on his face. There was a damp chill in the air, an ancient, evil staleness in his nostrils. Modern steel hooks were set in the wall, and there was a rope ladder lying bundled to one side. 'Can't you light it?'

The caretaker nodded. 'I did – he asked me to put them off again. He's been used to the dark – the lights hurt his eyes.'

Thane strode over to the dark hole and looked down into its gaping black unreality. 'Down there . . . we're going to get you out. We're putting on the lights first. All right?'

'Yes – yes, I'm ready.' The voice was shaky, with a near hysterical edge of relief to it.

'Now, then.' Thane nodded to the caretaker. The man flicked a switch beside him, and a circle of bare electric bulbs snapped to life in the pit below. In the foot of the bottle, the man who crouched on the rock threw up an arm to cover his eyes. But the momentary glimpse was enough for the two detectives above . . . they'd found Peter Herrald.

With practised ease the caretaker came forward, fitted the rope ladder to its hooks, and let it uncoil down into the pit. Phil Moss was first down its swaying length, the caretaker gave Thane a steadying hand over the rim of the edging wall, and in seconds all three were down beside the prisoner.

Gently, Moss drew the man's arm away from his face. 'It's over now, Mr Herrald.'

Peter Herrald kept his eyes closed against the light. His face had a thick stubble of beard beneath its grime, his thinning fair hair was unkempt, and he kept his hands clasped tight against the crumpled cloth of his soiled grey sports jacket. He licked his lips and took a deep, sighing breath. 'I –' He stopped and shook his head. 'How did you find me?'

'Mostly luck.' Thane stared around him in fascination. Plenty of old castle fortresses in Europe could still show examples of the incompassionate savagery with which prisoners had been treated in the Dark Ages of history, places now seen only occasionally by the student or the tourist who went poking beyond the bright lights of the holiday centres. But this one – to a native Scot it was a sobering revelation of the ways of his ancestors.

The bottle dungeon had been hacked out of the living rock on which the castle was built. Its 'neck' was a circular shaft some eight feet in depth and five feet across, the black band of the coal seam clearly visible against the paler sandstone. Then below the neck, the bottle widened, its sides flaring outwards all around for another fifteen feet, the final pit being fifteen feet across – and its floor sloping in from the walls to form a shallow, cone-shaped depression. Once down here, no man living could ever have escaped again unaided . . . down here, in the dark and the damp and the silence.

The castle caretaker had seen the same reaction many a time before.

'Aye, it's no' a very pleasant place,' he mused. 'And many a poor devil found that out. A few years and they'd go blind or daft or both.' There was worry on his face as he looked back to Herrald. 'What's going to happen about – about him?'

'A lot.' Thane bent down beside Herrald, who had now opened his eyes a fraction but still shielded them against the light. 'When did they bring you here?'

'The same day they killed George Shaw.' Herrald shuddered and swallowed hard. 'You know about that?'

'Most of it.' Thane studied the manufacturer's agent for a moment. Over three days in this damp blackness of a pit – Peter Herrald appeared to have paid heavily for his quixotic offer to help these runaway trawlermen. 'Can you tell me where they are now? Did you hear them talk?'

'Talk?' Herrald's laugh trembled as it echoed round the stone walls. 'Since they put me here, I've been alone most of the time. They'd come and feed me, that's about all. Sometimes there was one of them just standing up above, listening . . .' His voice sank to a near whimper. 'I tried shouting at first, then pleading with them. But it didn't make any difference.'

Phil Moss gave a grunt. 'Half a dozen men could shout their heads off down here and they wouldn't be heard outside. Come on, let's try you on your feet.' The castle caretaker helped him bring Herrald up from his crouch.

'Did they tell you they were going to kill Shashkov?' Thane probed on, still hopeful that this crumpled, unshaven figure might be able to give him some lead.

'Kelch said so – that was after George found the gelignite and wanted to turn them in to the police. That – that was why they killed him, to stop him.' He looked round the three rescuers. 'Could one of you give me a cigarette?'

Thane fumbled in his pocket, then remembered he'd none. The caretaker filled the gap, and the manufacturer's agent cupped his grimy hands round the match as it flared.

'Thanks. I . . . they took mine. Took everything.' He drew in a long pull of the smoke and let it trickle slowly from his nostrils.

'General Shashkov is still intact. Right now he's playing golf about a mile from here.' Thane rubbed his chin. 'Listen, Herrald, this is vital. Did you hear anything, anything at all, about what they were going to do?'

'Me?' Slowly, Herrald shook his head. 'Don't you understand? I don't know anything.' There was an open pleading in his voice. 'Don't you understand? I don't know where this place is, I don't know what time it is except that it's probably still Saturday. The one who was here just before you came – Bretsun, I think it was – he told me they were going away, and that I'd be found in a day or so. He was starting to say something else, then he seemed to realize something was wrong. He went out, I heard voices, and I began shouting again . . . that's all I know.'

'All right, take it easy.' Thane tried to hide his disappointment. 'Can you make it up that ladder if we help?'

Herrald gave a twisted grin. 'I – I'll make it. If it gets me out of here, I'll make it.'

The caretaker went up first. Herrald came next, with Phil Moss close behind, helping him from rung to rung. Thane came last of all, grunting at the twinging pain from his shoulder, grateful for the heave of assistance his wiry second-in-command gave him as he reached the top.

'The light still hurts.' Peter Herrald screwed his eyes shut as he looked out at daylight for the first time.

'It'll pass.' Thane urged him gently through the outer door, and breathed deep, the fresh salt sea air like nectar after the stagnating atmosphere of the pit. 'A bath, a shave, a change of clothes and a decent meal and you'll feel a darned sight better.' He could see an ambulance drawn up outside the castle, and a second police car. As they walked slowly out into the courtyard a small procession came from the opposite side of the old building, a stretcher carried in their midst.

One of the men detached himself from the group and hurried over. The county sergeant gave a hasty salute as he approached. 'We've got him off now, sir. But the doctor says he hasn't much chance.'

'Still unconscious?'

'And likely to stay that way, it seems.' The sergeant ran a finger round the inside of his shirt collar. 'He's in a bit o' a mess, sir. Eh – should you no' be seeing about that shoulder o' yours? We're taking him to the hospital. You could come along, too, an'' – he glanced significantly at

144

Herrald – 'it might be an idea to take him along while we're at it.'

Thane rubbed his shoulder, thought for a moment, then nodded. 'Take him with you. I'll come as soon as I've got word to Colonel Donnan. All quiet on the course?'

'So far, sir.' The sergeant gave a flickering grin. 'I heard one of our lads on the car radio while I was waitin' for the ambulance, an' it's quite a game. Thon Russian took nine strokes at the first hole and a ten at the second – he's thumping that wee ball as if it was the original enemy of the people!' He stepped over to Herrald and took him by the arm. 'Now then, come an' –' He froze, the rest of it dying on his lips as a low, flat thunder-like roar split the quiet of the courtyard.

They turned instinctively, though the castle's tumble-down walls and the curve of the shore-line both cut off any chance of seeing the Old Course. Thane had a momentary glimpse of one of the helicopters beating a hurried way across the sky, then it, too, was gone from view.

Phil Moss gave a soft sigh. 'That was a big 'un!'

Thane gave a slow nod, all expression wiped from his face, a tight ball of tension gripping within him. Then, moving by sheer instinct, they were both sprinting towards the castle gateway.

It took their car two minutes in a flat-out siren-wailing rush to reach the Old Course, and just over that time to push on down the road which bounded the first leg of its landward side, where every few yards blue-uniformed police or khaki-clad army men stood staring towards the green horizon line. As the road petered out at the side of a collection of railway sheds, the driver licked his lips and glanced sideways at Thane.

'Keep going!'

The man nodded, dropped his speed, changed gear, and swung the wheel as he saw his chance. Heaving and swaying, the car bucked a way over the fringe of rough ground bordering the road. Springs thudded a protest, and then the tyres were running in a soft whisper over the smooth turf of the course. They gained speed again, threading their swaying path past bunkers, leaving the fluttering flag of the second hole behind, braking hard at the top of one rise at the side of the fold in the ground beyond. The car's tyres spun for a moment as it was urged in a new direction and then they were on their way once more.

General Shashkov's golfing expedition were gathered in a group at the fourth tee . . . and apart from the guns in the hands of the tense, grim-faced ring of security guards there was no sign of trouble in the party. Thane could see the Soviet Minister of Industrial Development's green windcheater moving among a small, closely-clustered group of figures standing to one side of the ring.

As the car stopped, Thane threw open his door and leaned out. 'Where's Colonel Donnan?'

The nearest of the guards, a thin, ginger-haired six-footer with a straggling moustache, used the muzzle of his loosely-held Patchett gun as a pointer. 'On his way back now . . . he went on up to have a look at whatever it was that went bang.'

Thane got out of the car and followed the line of the gun muzzle. One of the helicopters was whirring back towards them, its rotors scything a shimmering disc against the blue sky. A moment later it came in low, hovered noisily, then swept a miniature dust storm to life as it settled to land about fifty yards away. While the rotors slowed to a quieter tick-over, Colonel Donnan's small plump form jumped from the cabin and came trotting over.

The little Irishman, his face a determined pink, gave the briefest of nods. 'Hold on – I'll be right back.'

He passed Thane at the same steady trot, heading straight for General Shashkov's waiting group. An interested spectator, Phil Moss emerged from the car and stood beside Thane to watch what followed. Whatever Donnan was saying, Shashkov obviously didn't like it. A young, anxious-faced interpreter standing between them, the little Irishman and the bulky, gaily-attired Communist engaged in a growing rumble of conversation, both brushing aside any interruptions from the others around.

At last, it ended. General Shashkov spun on his heel, barked at his followers, and the entire party began trekking back the way they had come – all, that was, except his opponent who was left standing, idly swinging a club in undecided fashion. After a moment, he too began to walk slowly away.

'And that's ruddy well that.' There was a look of grim-jawed satisfaction on the security chief's face as he stumped over to the police car. Then he stopped short as, for the first time, he noticed Thane's arm. 'Hey, what happened to you?'

'One of Kelch's pals – Arkan Bretsun. We've recovered Peter Herrald, too. They had him stowed away in a hell-hole corner of that castle.'

Donnan gave a mild curse, his mind only half-occupied by the information. 'The obvious again – so obvious everybody dam' well overlooks it,' he said bitterly. 'The same on ahead. A squad of men check over every conceivable place with mine detectors, straining for the slightest signal that there's any metal buried – and come back with half a dozen ancient horseshoes and a load of old iron. Yet they miss a bomb planted right under their ruddy noses!'

'What happened?' It was Thane's turn to ask.

Donnan shrugged. 'Come and see for yourself. I'm going back up anyway. Shashkov's heading straight for the club-house. I told him he either went back under his own steam or we ruddy well carried him.'

'Diplomatically, or just like that?' Phil Moss raised one cynical eyebrow.

'More or less like that.' Donnan scuffed one foot on the turf. 'There's a harmless old character lying dead out there just because our ruddy V.I.P. wouldn't take "niet" for an answer till now.' He gestured towards the helicopter. 'Well, coming, Thane? You too, Moss, if you like.'

Phil Moss shook his head. 'Not in that thing. Unless . . .' He looked questioningly at Thane and relaxed as the Millside chief shook his head.

'Take the car back, Phil. Make sure the roadblocks stay on their toes, and start organizing another comb-out of the town. If Kelch and Stender know they've failed, then find we've located Herrald and knocked off Bretsun, they're liable to try to make a break for it.'

'If they haven't done it already.' Resigned to his task, his second-in-command watched the two men go over to the helicopter and scramble aboard. Then, as the rotors quickened and the machine rose, he turned back to the car. His stomach rumbled ominously as he settled into the passenger seat, and he sighed as he reached for his pill-box.


The 'copter pilot, a gum-chewing R.A.F. man, swung his machine in a tight turn as it climbed, then sent it heading north only a hundred feet or so above the ground.

'First time?' bellowed Donnan above the beating roar.

Thane nodded, watching the smooth fairways ripple past below like some giant, close-woven carpet. 'Where are we heading?'

'The tenth hole – what's left of it.' Donnan pointed over to his right, down to where the Old Course's fringe of rough merged with the longer grass and sand dunes leading to the shore, where the waves were coming in whitecapped and steady. 'But take a look over there first. This old boy – his name was Wallace – had a set-to with the police on duty at the first tee earlier this morning. I know that part because the cop concerned mentioned it to one of my men and described the old fellow. Treated it as a joke, which is all it was then. Anyway, he chased him off. But it looks as though the old fellow had a stubborn streak in him, and sneaked out along the shore with his clubs –

there's a road running right along, and we couldn't close the beach to holidaymakers, not without having a riot on our hands. Doing it to the course was bad enough!'

'But there was a cordon . . .' protested Thane.

'Who were too busy watching for an organized invasion to spot one old man who knew his way around.' Donnan scowled. 'Anyway, he got on to the course at the ninth hole, just where it starts to turn and come back. The soonest we knew he was there was when one of the helicopters radioed that there was a character happily golfing his way along the tenth fairway! I chased the nearest squad I had towards him, but they were too late.' He slammed one clenched fist into the other. 'Too late, Thane – and the shame of it is I should be glad they were, glad the old gent blew himself sky high!'

'Otherwise it might have been Shashkov who went up.' Thane said it quietly. It wasn't his job to hold the scales, but it was easy enough to sympathize with the practical viewpoint. 'Where was the bomb?'

'In the hole – in the ruddy hole.' Donnan moaned at the thought. 'And there's the result.' He pointed below again, at the same time as the helicopter began to lose height.

The tenth green, set higher than the fairway which led to it and with a tricky backward slope which had beaten many a championship exponent, was now disfigured by a dark brown crater of dislodged earth eighteen to twenty feet from edge to ragged edge. A handful of men, some in civilian clothes, two in khaki with an Alsatian dog beside them, stood watching the helicopter descend. A coat was spread over the face and upper body of the dead man lying near them.

Thane and Donnan left the machine as soon as it touched down and crossed over to the others, who waited with a professional lack of curiosity.

'Found anything more?' asked Donnan.

'Just this, sir.' One of the dog-handlers showed a round,

blackened object, barely recognizable as a golf ball. 'It was over by those whin bushes, about forty yards away.'

'You saw it happen?' Thane had bent down beside the body. Now he replaced the coat and rose. From the extent of his injuries, the old man must have been killed instantly.

'That's right, sir.' The dog-handler scratched his charge lightly behind one ear. 'We got a message someone was over here and started across. When we saw the bloke, my mate gave a shout, but he just played his next shot on to the green as if he'd never heard us.'

'And a minute later the thing blew up,' said Donnan wearily.

The dog-handler nodded. 'He'd chipped his ball fairly close to the pin, maybe four or five feet away. While we were still coming over, he took the flag pin from the hole, picked up his putter, and knocked the ball in – a perfect putt. The place exploded the same second.'

'And the ball came out of that can again as if it had been shot from a gun.' The Alsatian cocked its ears as Thane whistled tunelessly through his teeth. 'I see what you mean, Colonel. They took out the regular can at the hole, dug down a bit more, then replaced the can with their own version, complete with gelignite attached beneath. It could have been done any time last night, and in theory –'

'In theory, the first golfers to reach the hole today should have been Shashkov and his partner,' said the little security chief. 'It took a stubborn old man to upset the apple-cart.'

The only tricky part of the scheme would be building the firing mechanism, and even that would have posed no major problem to a handyman, decided Thane. Given a few simple tools, the type of materials which could be obtained in almost any bicycle shop and a few hours for trial and error experiment, the finished product could be guaranteed almost foolproof. It had probably been a two-stage system, stage one a 'safety-catch' released when the flag pin was removed from the hole, stage two a spring-balanced bottom plate with a battery-electric contact, the circuit to the detonator completed by the sheer weight of the golf ball dropping into the hole.

Of course, a fluke long-distance putt could have wrecked the scheme. But neither Shashkov nor his opponent were in the Ben Hogan class . . . yes, the basic courtesies of the game would have taken care of the rest. Both men would have been within the killing circle when the blast occurred.

'We'll keep an eye on things here until your boffin squad can get here.' Donnan's voice cut across his thoughts. 'Anything else you'll need?'

'Statements – but there's no hurry. And the course will have to stay closed for the rest of the day.'

'That's a police job now.' Donnan shook his head. 'I've got troubles enough – and the press relations boys at Whitehall are going to have nightmares over this one.'


The helicopter whisked them back to the clubhouse and from there a car took Thane on to the local hospital. Twenty minutes later, his shoulder wound cleaned and bandaged, wearing a fresh shirt and a sports jacket loaned by one of the hospital residents to replace his own slashed and blood-stained garments, a fresh package of cigarettes in his pocket, he felt ready for work again.

'A simple enough wound.' Professor MacMaster, an interested observer throughout the treatment, seemed almost disappointed. The forensic expert was still smarting at the way he'd been handled before he'd been able to get through the cordon at the clubhouse. 'A week or two should be enough for complete healing, which is more than can be said for the man who caused it.'

'I heard.' Arkan Bretsun was dead. Still unconscious when he reached the hospital, he'd lasted barely minutes thereafter – no medical skill could have saved him.

'No sense in blaming yourself.' MacMaster mellowed a little. 'None at all. Why isn't Inspector Moss around?'

'There are still two of them on the loose,' reminded Thane. 'He's trying to find them.'

'Well, I've a task of my own waiting' – MacMaster rose to go – 'a visit to the golf course before they remove Wallace's body. I'd better leave you this.' He produced one of his familiar wax-sealed envelopes. 'It's the report I mentioned to Laurence, fingerprints found at the cottage.'

'Thanks.' Thane moved his arm experimentally. It was stiff, and the bandages were restricting, but he felt little pain. Once MacMaster had left, he put the envelope in his pocket and rose to his feet. It was time for a talk with Peter Herrald.

A nurse in the corridor outside the casualty office guided him along to the room where the manufacturer's agent was a restless patient. The hospital's opinion was that Herrald needed a spell of rest and quiet, but he had a different view. Sitting up in bed, wearing a heavy, hospital-issue dressing-gown over pyjamas, the promised bath, shave and hot meal seemed to have considerably raised his spirits.

'You're looking better, anyway,' Thane agreed.

'I'm fine, just a bit weak at the knees.' The other man grimaced. 'And I don't like hospitals – don't ask me why, I just don't. The sergeant who brought me here promised he'd find me some clean clothes. As soon as he does, I'm getting out – no matter what they say.' He hesitated. 'Eh . . . I hope you don't mind, Chief Inspector, but I made a phone call a few minutes ago.'

'Depends who you were calling.' Thane sat on the edge of the bed and took out his cigarettes. 'Lady Dunspar and her daughter Barbara?'

'That's right.' Herrald gave a slightly sheepish grin. 'I felt – well, you know . . .' He took one of the cigarettes, then a light, and settled back against the pillows.

'I know you're pretty friendly with them.' Thane lit his

152

own cigarette and found an ashtray. 'What I want to do now is fill in some of the gaps. We know Lady Dunspar telephoned you on the Friday evening and told you Kelch and the others had turned up at her home. What happened then?'

Herrald sighed. 'I said I'd help, which was the biggest mistake I've ever made – but it seemed right at the time.'

'Why'd you ask her not to tell her daughter?'

'Just wanted to keep her out of it.' Herrald shrugged. 'You know, in case there was . . . well, trouble later. Not that I thought there would be. I'd pretty well worked out how to do it when her mother phoned again on the Saturday. Freighter on one of the South American runs – easier to get ashore at the other end, and they could work their own way north from there.'

Thane rubbed his chin. 'Did Shaw know what you were up to?'

'No. Not at first. We'd fixed up the fishing trip, we were going north anyway.' Herrald shifted uncomfortably then drew hard on the cigarette. 'All I planned to do was help some poor devils out of their troubles.'

'Right. Let's take it stage by stage. When Lady Dunspar phoned again on the Saturday, before you left, you arranged to meet Kelch. Where and when?'

'On the Tuesday evening, outside the Tayman Hotel at Aberfeldy.'

'Where were you till then?'

'Fishing.' Herrald appeared puzzled. 'Why?'

'I'm just trying to fill in the picture,' said Thane patiently. 'Where did you camp the first night? Near Stirling?'

'No, we drove right up to Loch Tay and camped there, in a clearing just off the road – George Shaw had been there before.'

'When did you tell him what was going on?'

'On the Tuesday afternoon. He – well, he wasn't very happy about it at first, but I told him he didn't need to get involved to any real extent and he said it would be all right as long as his wife didn't find out.' Herrald bit his lip. 'We treated it as a bit of a lark.'

'So the first time you met Kelch was that evening. What happened?'

'Well, he seemed a decent enough character, bitter at times, but we expected that. We arranged to drive up to the old cottage where they were hiding out first thing the next morning. I'd a camera with me, and I wanted to get their photographs and some other details –'

'Fake travel documents?'

'Well, passes, that sort of thing.' Herrald's voice was becoming slightly strained. 'Look, I haven't done this before, if that's what you're hinting. But you get to know the ropes. Anyway, we went up as arranged and they were friendly enough. We talked it over and had some food with them – and then George found the explosives. Two boxes of the stuff and some detonators – it was an accident the way it happened. They had them wrapped up in sacking and lying in a corner. George was nosing about, and saw what the stuff was before they could stop him.'

Thane nodded. So far, the story was falling pretty well into the shape he'd expected. 'And the row began,' he prompted.

'That's right. George – well, he began asking questions, wanting answers. Kelch told him to forget what he'd seen –'

'What about you?'

Herrald shook his head. 'I kept quiet. George was doing enough talking for us both, anyway. Then he marched across to the van and shouted to me to come too, that he was going for the police. That was when Kelch pulled the gun but George must have thought he was bluffing, because he got in and slammed the door. Next second Kelch fired at him through the window.'

'What happened to you?'

'They shoved me back in the cottage and kept me there. When they brought me out again they told me how – what they'd done about George, and that they were making it look as if I'd panicked and made a bolt for it.'

'I see.' Thane stubbed his cigarette, rose from the bed and walked across to the window. The hospital gardens were in full bloom, a riot of colours. 'That's when they told you about Shashkov?'

'Kelch did. He was running the show – though the others didn't need much pushing. As far as Kelch was concerned, nothing else seemed to matter.'

'Not even losing his chance to get abroad?' Thane turned from the window. 'How did he hope to get away? Still use you?'

'It didn't seem to matter any more. I told you.' Herrald took a last, nervous puff at his cigarette. 'Then they took my keys, my wallet, everything. Kelch said he knew a place where they could keep me out of the road and lie low themselves if they had to – he'd found it when he was looking over the places Shashkov would visit. They gathered their kit together, tied me up, and shoved me in the boot of the Ford. Then the car drove off. Hours it seemed to last, and there must have been either fumes getting in, or the air became used up. Anyway, I passed out. When I came to I was in that – that pit. That's all I know.'

Thane nodded. 'And that's all I'll ask for now. Oh . . . except this. In case we want to contact you, what are your plans once these clothes arrive?'

'Get out of here, have a couple of stiff whiskies, then wait for Barbara and her mother to arrive – they're driving over. They want me to go back with them and rest up for a few days.'

'Sounds sensible.' Thane gave him a brief farewell nod and left the room, closing the door behind him. Outside, he stopped to light another cigarette then saw the big red No Smoking sign on the wall ahead and ruefully tucked the packet away again. He walked on along the corridor, towards the main door of the hospital – then stopped short as it swung open and Phil Moss strode in.

'I hoped you'd still be here.' Moss's voice was grey and colourless, his manner tired and yet somehow relieved. 'We don't need to look for Martin Kelch any more.'

'He's been picked up?' Thane's first reaction was surprise. 'Where?'

'He's been located.' Moss chose the words with professional care. 'A couple of youngsters found him down by the harbour, Colin. He was lying in a corner, behind a pile of old fish boxes – and the gun was still in his hand.'

'Suicide?' Thane winced. All else apart, he somehow hadn't pictured the trawlerman taking that way out.

'A good try at it. Maybe good enough yet.' Moss jerked a thumb over his shoulder. 'The ambulance is bringing him in now. He's got a bullet through his head, but he's still alive – for the moment, and only just.' He pursed his lips. 'I'd say the rest is a formality, but they're going to try to operate.'

Make him well enough to hang was what he meant, and they both knew it. Thane cursed softly and blindly. 'Can he talk?'

His second-in-command shook his head. 'The only way you'd know he was still with us is via a stethoscope. I've kept the search going for Stender.'

Three down now, and one to go. But Stender was small beer compared with Martin Kelch.

'What now, Colin?' Moss asked it for a second time before Thane came back to realities.

'You've got someone with him?'

'One of the local C.I.D. men – with orders to stick beside him right through.'

'Right.' They were part of a machine, a machine with a job to do, one it had done hundreds of times before, often enough to be second nature to all its individual parts. 'Let's go and have a look at the place, Phil.'

They left the hospital just as the ambulance arrived.

# Chapter Eight

It was quiet, almost peaceful down by the tiny, old-fashioned harbour. The ambulance's arrival and departure had been seen by only a handful of people and, the excitement apparently over, most of them had drifted away.

'Over here. . . .' Moss led the way as they left the car and walked along the quayside. It was low tide, and most of the collection of fishing boats and small pleasure craft which occupied the harbour's area were either high and dry on the exposed sandy bottom or sitting at an angle in the shallow water. The harbour itself was little more than a long stone breakwater and a flanking quayside, a base for motor boat trips round the bay and a haven from the waves which could batter so furiously along that stretch of the North Sea coastline.

The uniformed man left on guard saluted as they approached the small mountain of fish boxes lying near the junction of breakwater and quay. Beside him, two youths in heavy roll-necked jerseys and faded blue jeans showed immediate interest.

'These are the lads who found him,' explained Phil Moss. 'Johnny MacVey and –'

'Sandy Porter,' nodded the second of the pair, a brief grin crossing his freckled face. 'Who's your pal, Inspector?'

'My name's Thane.' He took an immediate liking to the pair – their easy, frank appearance made a welcome, refreshing contrast to the average run of the past few days.

'You've told the story before, I know. But I'd like to hear it myself.'

The two youngsters glanced at one another and Porter scratched his head. 'It's not much of a story. We're up from Edinburgh for the week-end, to do a spot of skin-diving. Our gear's over in the car.' He gestured towards an old but well-polished Vauxhall, parked a little way along the quayside. 'Anyway, we reached the harbour about twenty minutes ago – the idea was to try exploring along the outer line of the breakwater. Changing into underwater kit in a car is possible but pretty cramping – so we thought we'd try and find a sheltered spot around here.'

'And this was it?'

'We thought so.' The youngster grimaced. 'Instead, we found the bloke lying in behind the boxes. Johnny waited here and I went off to phone the police. But I didn't have to – I bumped into a couple of 'em before I reached a telephone.'

'Two of the local men,' explained Moss. 'I had them keeping an eye around the harbour, just in case Kelch and his pal tried to pinch a boat.'

'One way of getting round the roadblocks,' acknowledged Thane. He turned back to the skin-divers. 'Did either of you hear any noise, see anything before you found him?'

The two youngsters shook their heads.

'But the gun was still in his hand,' volunteered the hitherto silent partner.

'Constable?'

The uniformed man cleared his throat. 'We've asked around, sir. With the tide out, the harbour was pretty well deserted. But there were some folk on one of those boats – the cabin cruiser with the yellow hull lying across the harbour. They say they heard some sort of noise like a shot, and from their story it would be about ten or fifteen minutes before these lads came along. That's all they know, sir. They looked out, right enough – they'd heard the bang from the Old Course beforehand and were wondering what was happening. But they didn't see anything.'

'Nobody did,' said Moss, his face tight with annoyance. 'It was the same story from the bunch I asked before I went up to the hospital.'

Thane shrugged his acceptance. 'We'll need you along at the police office later, for a formal statement, but that's all for now,' he told the two skin-divers.

They nodded then headed off towards their car, their expedition temporarily abandoned.

'Got the cartridge case, Phil?' Thane knelt to examine the dark red pool of blood staining part of the worn stone of the quayside in the shadowed space behind the crates.

'In my pocket,' confirmed his second-in-command. 'It was lying beside one of the boxes – I've marked the place. But the bullet must still be around.'

'Exit wound?' Thane anticipated his companion's nod of agreement. At such close range, a nine millimetre bullet's velocity was savage to behold.

Together, they made a gradually widening search for the missing metal slug. They finally located it, flattened and almost beyond recognition – the obvious result of a ricochet from part of the stonework around.

From the harbour, they went back to the hospital and arrived at its entrance just as Peter Herrald was about to step into a waiting taxi. The manufacturer's agent was leaning shakily on the arm of a nurse, but there was a look of determination on his face. He saw them, stopped, and gave a smile as they approached.

'I told you I'd be out of here as soon as I got some clothes.'

Colin Thane ran an eye over the new but ill-fitting suit Herrald was wearing. 'How is he, nurse?'

The nurse gave a shrug. 'The doctor wanted him to stay, sir, but Mr Herrald has voluntarily discharged himself –'

'And they can't keep me. But thanks for what you've done.' Herrald ran one hand over the sleeve of his jacket.

'As soon as I get some cash I'll need to settle up with the outfitter who supplied this.'

'Better take some money while you're at it – pay me back later.' Thane took out his wallet and gave Herrald four of the one pound notes it contained.

'Thanks.' Herrald gratefully pocketed the cash. 'I've already borrowed something from the doctor who tried to keep me in – add this, and I'm solvent for the moment.' He ran his tongue lightly over his lips. 'I – I heard about Kelch. Is that why you're back?'

Thane nodded.

'Seems they don't think much of his chances. Well, personally I won't lose any sleep over it,' Herrald gave a tight grin. 'Do you blame me?' Without waiting for an answer he got aboard the taxi. The door slammed shut and in a moment it was driving off.

As the vehicle swung out through the hospital gates the two detectives followed the nurse into the building. The young doctor who'd dressed Thane's shoulder wound was still on duty – and could tell them right off that their trip had been a waste of time.

'They're working on him in theatre, and probably will be for about another hour,' he declared.

'How does it look?'

'Nasty. But beyond that I don't know what the chances are.'

'We'll come back. But if anything happens before we do . . .'

'We'll whistle you up, don't worry,' he assured them.

When they got back to the police station, a waiting swarm of figures descended on the car.

'Gentlemen of the press,' said Moss wryly. 'Like flies round a honeypot.' Reluctantly, he opened the car door and was first out. A moment later, he gave an indignant hoot. 'Get these ruddy cameras out from under my nose!'

The cameramen fell back, their task completed. As they went, the notebook brigade swung forward.

'Sorry boys.' Thane glanced round the circle, recognizing several familiar faces. 'There's no statement coming from me. Maybe later –'

'From a Ministry spokesman?' The cynical query, from a tall, rabbit-jawed character he recognized as Scottish stringer for one of the London nationals, brought a sardonic chuckle from the others. 'General Shashkov's put out a statement about the bomb attempt, Chief Inspector. It roasts everybody from the British Government downwards.' He flipped through the pages of his notebook. 'What about this? "It is hard to see how such an outrage could have occurred unless there had been definite and perhaps even deliberate negligence of elementary safeguards." Don't you want to answer it?'

'That's not my job at the moment.' Thane began to push his way through the clustering group, his face expressionless. It probably wouldn't be long before the pressmen got their first hint of what had been happening away from the Old Course, and when that happened the real hue and cry would begin. But this was one time when his usual reputation for being reasonably co-operative with the press was going to take a drastic beating.

Inside the police station, Phil Moss gave a sigh of relief as he slammed the door, shutting out the last protests from their pursuers. 'Another load of trouble round our necks.' His expression was gloomy.

'What else?' asked Thane. 'Shashkov was bound to make the most of it. But at least we'll get rid of him in one piece now.'

'There's still Stender left.'

'It's finished, Phil.' Thane was optimistic. 'All we've got now is one very frightened trawlerman, hiding somewhere and wondering how long it'll be before he's rounded up.'

162

They checked with the station duty officer, but that harassed individual had nothing fresh to report.

'Not unless you're interested in a character who couldn't remember where he left his car,' he grumbled. 'First he phones and says it's gone from where he left it last night, in the street round the corner from where he lives. I let the roadblocks know and put out a general alert . . . that was a quarter of an hour ago. Now he's just phoned again. He just found it, further along the same street.'

'Intact?' asked Thane.

'Yes. But he left it unlocked. Interested?'

'Better check on it, just in case,' Thane told him.

The duty officer could supply something more welcome – a mug of tea and a sandwich each.

'Ah . . .' Thane settled back in a chair in the same room they'd used most of the night, took a long gulp of the tea, then a first bite at the thick-cut bread. 'Twisted luck, that's all it's been, Phil. Twisted one way, then the other. Yet it wouldn't have happened at all if those four had jumped ship at any other time than when Shashkov was due here. They'd either have been whisked out of the country by Herrald or would have ended up walking into a police station somewhere and asking for a bed for the night.'

'I wonder why Kelch did it – shoot himself, I mean.' Moss tasted the tea. It was strong and tarry, and what it was going to do to his digestive acids he hated to imagine.

'Looks plain enough.' Thane chewed for a moment. 'The Old Course must have been their last big effort – the one that wouldn't fail. But it did, which was a big enough blow for him. On top of that, supposing Kelch had a rendezvous with the others down at the harbour once the blast was over and they'd gathered an idea of what happened. Your own idea fits, that they were planning to pinch a boat. If he passed the castle and saw the place cluttered with cops he'd know we'd found Herrald. Then Bretsun doesn't turn up, and he gets worried. Supposing Stender is missing, too, because he's too busy dodging our patrols to be able to make it?'

'Leaving Kelch alone with a complete failure and a double indictment for murder hanging over him,' murmured Moss. 'Not a pleasant future.'

'Plus one thing more,' said Thane, running his fingers round the edge of the tea mug. 'It was low tide, Phil . . . a damn fool mistake for a fisherman to make, but that's how it happens. The odds were that any of the boats he could handle on his own were stuck high and dry.'

'And so to a bullet in the head.' Moss finished his sandwich, abandoned the tea, and lit a cigarette. 'What's that?'

Ruefully, Thane contemplated the envelope in his hand. 'A present from Professor MacMaster. Well, we won't have much need of it now, but let's see anyway.' He ripped open the flap, took out the folded, typewritten sheets within, and glanced through them. Suddenly he stopped, frowned, then went back to the beginning of the report and read it through again from start to finish. The frown deepened. Then he passed the sheets across to his second-in-command. 'Read it, Phil. Carefully.'

Detective Inspector Moss obeyed. When he was finished, he was just as puzzled as he'd been at the start.

'Bacterial activity, chemical change . . .' He shook his head in bewilderment. 'Old MacMaster's been having fun, but what's it all about?'

Thane took back the papers. 'One point, Phil. A small one, but one I can't understand.' He glanced at the report again. 'Translated into plain English, MacMaster got hold of those emptied tins and other junk we found in the cottage where Shaw was killed.'

'I can read,' grunted Moss. 'Dan Laurence's boys found fingerprints on them, but that didn't surprise anyone.'

'It's the next part that matters, Phil.' Thane eyed him patiently. 'Some of the food they'd dumped was going bad.'

'And smelled like it.' Moss wrinkled his nose in remembered disgust.

'Belt up and listen for a minute, will you?' Thane rubbed his chin. 'MacMaster examined each item. Now listen. "Bacterial activity commences the moment any foodstuff is exposed to the air, as does chemical change . . . blah, blah . . . an interesting specimen was a glass jar which appeared to have contained a variety of meat paste".' He grinned to himself. 'That's what the ruddy label said, anyway. Here's what matters – "smeared traces of paste on the outer surface of the jar had been exposed for sufficient time to allow development of a characteristic mould growth". The rest of it . . .'

'Says that the mould grew over a part of the jar where Dan Laurence's boys found a fingerprint, or at least part of one,' nodded Moss, still uncertain but his interest growing. 'The print was partly eaten over by the mould but –' He broke off, mouth open in surprise as the situation percolated through.

'But could still be identified.' Thane's voice was a low murmur. MacMaster's report said the mould would have needed approximately four days to develop. Four days back from the time the jar had been collected by him meant the Monday.

Yet how could that whiskering blue-grey growth have been spreading across a fingerprint identified as Peter Herrald's when Herrald had told him that his first visit to the cottage hadn't been until the Wednesday?

As always, MacMaster's report was a masterpiece of caution. Temperature, humidity, a wide variety of factors could have influenced the mould's exact rate of development – but still left that four-day barrier. He summed up the situation as 'one of interesting research possibilities, so far untested by the courts.'

'Maybe Herrald picked up the jar on the Wednesday, when it had already been used?' Phil Moss strove for an easy explanation.

165

'No, that's out.' Thane rejected the suggestion with a degree of reluctance. 'According to MacMaster, the mould structure would show if that had happened – something to do with reaction on the sweat deposit from the skin pores.'

'Then Herrald either lied to you or was confused. Which?'

'He seemed certain enough.' Thane chewed his lip. 'We could go and ask him outright but – no, leave it just now. I'm more interested in Kelch.'

The hour crawled round with still no trace of Stender. The last of the runaways had performed a most efficient vanishing trick, and all Thane could do was make sure the local roadblock pattern was maintained and that the regular search network was in full operation in the areas beyond. Colonel Donnan telephoned from the manager's office at Sunbury Colliery . . . General Shashkov's visit there was going smoothly and without hitch, but the security chief was more interested in filling in the background to the fragmentary reports he'd been receiving.

Thane told him. When he'd finished, he heard the little Irishman give a sigh.

'I'll tell Shashkov. It won't make much difference to the build-up he's giving the whole affair, but I'll tell him. Once this visit is over we're heading back for Glasgow. You'll keep in touch?'

Thane promised and hung up. He looked at his watch, nodded to Phil Moss, and rose from his chair.


There was another visitor at the hospital when they arrived. Lady Dunspar, a lightweight fawn raincoat buttoned over her tweed costume, sat stubbornly in a chair in the waiting room a little way inside the entrance hall. Her face calm and determined, she glanced up as Thane's burly figure entered the room.

'There's little sense in being here,' he told her, his voice firm but sympathetic. 'I can't let you see him.'

'I know. The hospital staff said the same – that even if I did he wouldn't know I was there.' She shook her head. 'It doesn't matter. I – well, I can't explain, but I'll stay in this room until – well, until I'm forced to leave.'

'That's a matter for the hospital.' Thane understood, understood to a deeper extent than this proud, lonely woman would have believed. 'But if you're staying here, what about your daughter and Herrald?'

'I've told them.' Her eyes were troubled for a moment. 'It was difficult, very difficult, Chief Inspector. After what Martin did to Peter Herrald it may seem wrong for me to feel like this. Barbara said . . .' She pursed her lips. 'Anyway, they've changed their plans. Barbara is driving Peter back to Glasgow. They asked me to let you know.'

'I'll come back.' Thane left her and went out into the corridor. Phil Moss had apparently vanished, but as he glanced around, undecided, he heard footsteps and the small, wiry D.I. came round a corner towards him. At his side was an older, silver-haired man wearing a loose-hanging white hospital coat over an immaculate dark grey suit.

'Chief Inspector Thane?' The newcomer spoke with an underlying trace of North Country accent. 'I'm Gransden – surgical consultant. Your colleague tells me you want to hear anything I can tell you about the man Kelch's condition.'

'Anything possible,' agreed Thane.

'At this stage it doesn't amount to much.' The surgeon gestured them to follow and led the way back along the corridor. 'In here, I think . . .' He ushered them into a small, sunlit office and waited until they'd perched themselves on the long black leather couch which, with a desk and its chair plus a couple of filing cabinets, was the room's quota of furnishings. 'Now, how can I help?'

'The obvious question first. Will he live?'

'That would be the type of gambling forecast I abhor, Chief Inspector.' Gransden ran his thumbs over the tips of his scrubbed, close-cut fingernails and frowned. 'For the moment, the man's condition is critical. All we've done is – ah – what you might term a basic tidying up, emergency treatment. If we can and as soon as we can, we'll require to move him to a specialized neuro-surgical hospital. But to attempt that at the moment would be tantamount to killing him.'

'But you think he has a chance of pulling through?'

The surgeon shrugged. 'There's always a chance.' He gave a brief, frosty twinkle. 'You know, a bullet through the head isn't nearly as reliable a way of procuring death as the layman believes.'

'And in this case?' Thane gave a faint nod to his companion and Phil Moss dredged out notebook and pencil.

'The entry wound was in the temporal region, approximately here' – Gransden pointed with one forefinger to a spot just in front of and a little above his right ear – 'and the shot was fired at probably almost direct contact with the weapon. It was possible to see the muzzle outline in the powder tattooing on the skin. The bullet's passage from there was downwards and slightly forward, with the exit wound below the left antrum.' He gave the same wintery twinkle at Moss's slowing pencil. 'Below the cheekbone, Mr Moss. There's considerable damage around the region of the exit wound, of course – always is. And it's impossible yet to say what if any damage has been done to the optic nerves for a start.'

'But the brain is undamaged . . .' Thane raised a hopeful eyebrow.

'Apparently.' The surgeon was in pedantic mood. 'Even if it had been, the result wouldn't necessarily be fatal. There are certain – ah – spare areas in the cerebrum. But that's by the way. If he pulls through, a certain amount of repair work will be necessary.'

'He's still unconscious?'

'And likely to remain that way for some time to come,' confirmed Gransden. 'If you are really asking when, if he lives, you can have a chance at questioning him and getting any sort of a reply, then the answer could be several days.' He lost a little of his patience. 'The man's fighting for his life, Chief Inspector. The wound in itself would be bad enough without complications.'

'Sir?' Moss glanced up from his notebook. Colin Thane's face showed identical surprise.

The surgeon gave a tut of annoyance. 'The fellow was ill enough by any standard even before the gunshot wound.' He noticed their continued bewilderment and put the situation as simply as he could. 'Kelch is suffering from pneumonia, gentlemen. A fairly advanced case – pneumonic consolidation with a pleural effusion.'

It hit Thane with all the force of a blow to the stomach. 'How far advanced, Mr Gransden?'

'He must have been as weak as a kitten, running a very high temperature. My guess – only a guess, of course – is that the condition has been building for anything up to three days. He's in an oxygen tent at this moment, and in normal circumstances he should have been under medical care long before now.'

Colin Thane swallowed hard. 'I'd like as positive an answer as you can give me to this, sir. Could – could a man in that condition have been taking an active part in – well, in strenuous activities?'

Gransden chewed his lip and deliberated for a moment. 'That's difficult to say, damned difficult. Some people can keep going to the point of collapse. I'd say it would be possible but . . .' He shook his head.

'Can we see him?'

'No reason why not.' The surgeon began heading for the door.

'And one other request, sir. I'd like permission to have a paraffin wax test made of his right hand.'

The surgeon's eyes narrowed with fresh, thoughtful

interest. 'Like that, is it? All right. But it's only fair to warn you. I don't claim any vast experience, but the angle of the head wound, everything about it, is perfectly in accord with an attempted suicide. A little awkward, perhaps. But a last-second, involuntary movement of the head would account for both angle and failure.'

Once again they followed him.

The room where Martin Kelch was lying was one floor up. Outside the door, the county C.I.D. man rose from his chair as they approached.

'Nothing yet, sir.'

Thane nodded. Then, as the surgeon opened the door, he went in, Phil Moss just behind him.

Martin Kelch's bed was partly enveloped by the transparent cloak of the oxygen tent. As they entered, a nurse turned from the cylinders and controls placed to one side of the bed and glanced at Gransden.

'Carry on,' he told her. 'We'll only be a moment.'

The two Millside men moved forward and for the first time Thane saw the man he'd pursued so desperately . . . the man about whom he now had gathering doubt.

Bandages and heavy-padded dressings framed and obscured Martin Kelch's pale, thin, clean-shaven face. It was a delicately boned face, with wide mouth, firm chin and aquiline nose. His eyes were closed, the only sign that life still clung to him the almost imperceptible rise and fall of his chest.

'Satisfied?' The surgeon fidgeted impatiently.

'Yes.' Thane turned away from the bed. 'What happened to the clothes he was wearing?'

'Kept to one side, as Inspector Moss requested.'

The clothing was in a cupboard in a small ward utility room nearby. Gransden had his own work-schedule to maintain and was quite thankful to say goodbye as soon as he saw that they were finished with him. Once he'd gone, Thane turned to the little bundle.

'Just the pockets for now, Phil.'

By the time the last pocket had been emptied, the collection was slender, but still interesting.

The trousers yielded a heavy clasp knife, matches, a comb and some loose change. The overcoat added only a packet of cigarettes to the heap. But with the jacket Phil Moss had better luck. From the inside pocket he produced a thick bill-fold, and he whistled as he checked its contents. 'There's almost eighty quid here, Colin – and Herrald's driving licence!' He finished the other pockets, added a handkerchief, a ballpoint pen and some more loose change to the pile, then scratched his thinning hair. 'Well, what now? Look, it doesn't need a genius to guess what's on your mind, Colin. But even if we had twice as much to go on as we actually have, we'd still need to go easy, very, very easy.'

He waited, well aware of the struggle going on inside his burly, dark-haired friend – a struggle to weigh fact fairly against conviction, to balance a tightrope path between the urge to act on intuition and the knowledge that that could be just as dangerous as moving too slowly.

At last, Thane stirred. 'Phil, I want you to stay here for a spell. Organize the paraffin wax test and keep an eye on Kelch.'

'And you?'

'I'm heading for Glasgow. General Shashkov will be on his way there by now, and where Shashkov goes Colonel Donnan isn't far behind.'

'There's also the point that Peter Herrald will be back home this evening.' Moss's voice was dry and humourless. 'Thinking of having another little chat with him?'

A slow, equally humourless grin twisted one corner of Thane's mouth. 'Not yet, Phil. But I'm going to make sure that I know exactly where to find him if the time does come.' He pulled the bundle of clothing together. 'I'll take these with me – anything happens, contact me through Headquarters or the Division.'

'What about Lady Dunspar?'

'I promised I'd see her before I left. She's not likely to budge, Phil – it might be an idea to have a word with the matron and try and find her a more comfortable place.'

'I'll fix it.' As Thane left, his second-in-command slowly lit a cigarette. A thought struck him. It was almost two hours now since he'd last felt a twinge from his ulcer. It meant something, it always did. But he'd never yet managed to work out what or why.


Lady Dunspar was still sitting in the same chair in the downstairs waiting room. She got up as Thane entered, her eyes searching his face.

'You've seen him, Mr Thane?'

'A few minutes ago,' he told her. 'He's still unconscious, and likely to stay that way – and there's no sense pretending he isn't in a pretty bad way.'

'That's what they told me before.' She bit her lip. 'But . . . there's a chance, isn't there?'

'There always is.' Thane took the jacket from the bundle of clothing over his arm. 'Do you recognize this, Lady Dunspar?'

She glanced at it and shook her head.

'Do Herrald and your daughter know Martin Kelch is unconscious – how bad his condition is?'

'Yes. They – that was why Barbara was angry about my waiting. When the doctor told me it might be days before he came round, even if he won through, she – well, she said I was mad to stay, that it was unnatural after all that had happened.'

He left it at that, said goodbye, and went out. A few minutes later he was relaxing in the passenger seat of the same police Jaguar which had brought him north the night before. As the car ate the miles back towards Glasgow, the uniformed driver took a guarded glance towards his apparently sleepy-eyed passenger. The C.I.D. chief was usually a friendly, talkative character on a journey . . . well, he'd been putting in his share of overtime lately, he supposed.


It was late afternoon when the car reached the city. Thane spent a few minutes at Headquarters, just long enough to drop off the load of clothing at the Scientific Branch's outer office and to make a quick check through their file on the case. When he came out again, there was a new confidence in his step.

'Over to Millside now,' he told his driver. 'And let's get moving – I don't want to be grabbed by Buddha Ilford in search of explanations.'

The man grinned and obeyed, turning the car on to the fast dockside route across the city. In under ten minutes the Jaguar pulled to a halt outside the familiar, grimy bulk of the divisional police office.

Thane got out, headed non-stop through the public office, and climbed the stairs to the C.I.D. section. He nodded a greeting to the men on duty, but didn't slow until he'd reached the sanctuary of his own office. Once there, he back-heeled the door shut behind him, tossed his hat on to its peg, and dropped thankfully into the worn leather of the chair behind his desk. The hands of the clock on the opposite wall had still ten minutes to travel before they reached five p.m. – Saturday tea and television time in practically every home throughout the city. The Saturday sports editions of the evening newspapers would be starting their run on the presses as usual except that for once, their football news would have a challenge for front page supremacy in the Shashkov story.

There was one last cigarette left in his pack. He lit it, flicked the match away, then pulled a pad of scrap-paper towards him and began writing, marshalling into order the stepped sequence of moves he'd mentally roughed on the journey to the city.

When he'd finished, he stubbed the cigarette and lifted the telephone. The station switchboard girl came on the line almost immediately, surprise in her voice.

'Aye, I'm back,' he told her. 'But keep quiet about it. I'm still up north as far as most of the outside world is concerned.' He heard her chuckle, then went on. 'You're going to be kept pretty busy for a spell. First off, I want you to locate a Colonel Donnan – he's Home Office security and Headquarters should be able to tell you where he is about now. After that, get me a line through to the Army records section at Scottish Command.'

'Right, sir.'

'Oh – Jean.' He caught her just before she went off the line. 'Two other things, top priority. Give me a call to my home, will you? And any tea on the brew down in that cubby-hole of yours?'

'I'll cope – but we're low on sugar.'

Thane heard a buzz and a click, the pulse of the ringing tone over the line, then the receiver at the other end was lifted and his wife's voice answered.

'Just me, Mary. I'm back in town.'

'In one piece?' There was a strained brightness in her query. He'd heard it before – most policemen did when the pressure was on and things, unpleasant things, were happening.

'I'm fine. Well' – he glanced down at his shoulder – 'I've got a natty piece of bandaging as a decoration and you've got one shirt less to launder in future. How it happened was something separate. I'm telling you just in case you hear a different version.'

'Will you be home?'

'Tonight?' He knew she'd already guessed the answer. 'Not a chance, dear. But tomorrow, before noon. Kids okay?'

'They're both out playing.' She hesitated, 'Colin . . .'

'Don't bother saying it,' he assured her. 'The rough stuff's over. Okay now?'

'If you mean it.' But she didn't sound convinced.

They said goodbye and he replaced the receiver. Was the rough stuff really over? He'd said the same thing to Phil Moss, but then he'd been talking about Shashkov's safety. The rest – that would probably depend on exactly how carefully he handled what lay ahead.

A double knock sounded on the door of his room, and he looked up as it opened and Sergeant MacLeod came in.

. 'Spare a moment, sir?' MacLeod was cautious, with the memory of past experience of crisis times.

'Not much more than that, Mac.' He leaned back in the chair. 'But if you hadn't come I was on my way out to find you. How many men are free right now – or on jobs that can wait for a spell?'

The C.I.D. sergeant pursed his lips. 'Three, four including myself, sir – it's been reasonably quiet all day. Beech and Mahone will be clear as soon as they've booked in Vince Bruce.'

'Vince!' Thane gave a slow grin of appreciation at the news that the fleet-footed young burglar had finally been nailed. 'Who's our sprint star – Beech or Mahone?'

'Well, neither, sir.' MacLeod deliberately shifted his gaze towards the window. 'They were in the duty car when there was an emergency call to a housebreaking in Finlay Street. Vince made a break for it as they turned up, and jumped the back garden wall. But he landed badly, and sprained his ankle – they had to carry him in.'

Thane's grunt was comment enough. 'Anything else I should know?'

'The pitch-and-toss school, sir – Constable Newton reported in. He played last night, and he's going to be in the game again this evening. He says there's definitely another big game set for Sunday, but he won't know where it'll be until tonight. Do you still want the raid scheduled for tomorrow?'

'That's what I said and that's what I meant.' Thane

struggled against impatience. Being a divisional D.C.I. called for octopus-like abilities at any time, but right at that moment he could hardly have cared less about the pitch-and-toss gamblers. 'Did Newton say anything more?'

MacLeod gave a gloomy nod. 'He lost ten pounds last night, sir. But he reckons he'll collect some cash this time – something about a system he's trying.'

'That means he'll probably land the division in the bankruptcy court.' Thane sighed. 'Right, Mac, now here's –' He broke off with a frown as the telephone rang, shrugged, and answered it. But he brightened as he heard Colonel Donnan's voice sounding over the line.

'Unless it's important keep it brief, will you?' pleaded the little security man. 'I'm in Shashkov's suite at the Southern Hotel – and he's just announced he wants to go for a drive around town.'

'It's important. How soon can you get over to Mill-side?'

'Eh?' Donnan was bewildered.

'I said how soon can you get over.' Thane rammed each word over the wire. 'And the quicker the better. I don't think Kelch is the man we want.' He brushed aside the splutter which crackled over the line. 'I'll tell you why when I see you.'

He hung up on that, a smile wisping on his lips. Donnan would come all right. He glanced back to Sergeant MacLeod, standing patiently, his face expressionless.

'Your turn now, Mac.' He gave the C.I.D. man a brief, elementary sketch of the situation. 'I want a tail put on Herrald and the Mason girl. Use two men in case they split up later tonight.' He grunted at MacLeod's sardonic expression. 'Don't worry – they probably will. Tell who-ever are on it we'll relieve them if and when we can, but I'll have their guts if they lose contact, and a double helping if they're spotted.' He gave MacLeod the number of Barbara Mason's car, the hotel where she both worked and lived, Herrald's address. The rest boiled down to routine.

'I'll get them moving.' MacLeod turned towards the door.

'Not yet.' Thane pulled the scrap-pad towards him again. 'We're just getting started.'

It was another ten minutes before Detective Sergeant MacLeod finally emerged from Thane's room, ten minutes interrupted only by the arrival of an orderly with the promised tea from the switchboard, the same orderly's return with two packets of cigarettes, and a brief break when Thane's call to Army Records came through.

Outside, MacLeod closed the door gently behind him then looked around the main C.I.D. room, pursing his lips. Then he waved the half-dozen expectant, waiting men to gather around him. 'Tonight, just for once, you're going to have to work for your ruddy money,' he informed them. 'By tomorrow, most of you are going to wish you'd been drowned at birth. Now, let's get on with it.'


Colonel Donnan wasted a minimum of time in getting to Millside. But even so, only one detective was still in the main C.I.D. room when he arrived, an unfortunate d.c. trying to speak on two telephones at the same time while a third instrument pealed indignantly in the background. Donnan stalked past the confusion, rapped on Thane's office door, and barged in.

The Millside C.I.D. chief tossed down the pencil he'd been using and swung round in his chair to greet the security man.

'Well, you didn't waste time,' he declared, stoppering a chuckle as he saw the little Irishman's ruffled indignation. 'Sit down . . . cigarette, Colonel?'

The security chief ignored the offered packet and gave a sound close to a snarl. 'Never mind the social chit-chat, Thane. What the hell did you mean when you said Kelch wasn't the man we wanted? And if you thought it funny hanging up on me like that, I didn't . . . I'm damned if I did!'

'Couldn't think of a better way to get you here in double-quick time.' Thane met Donnan's glare, held it, and saw it die down a little as the man opposite recognized the iron-hard purpose which lay beneath the burly Millside detective's outward calm.

'Well . . .' He took the cigarette and a light. 'All right, I'll listen.'

'Start off with two factors, one of them a fingerprint.' Carefully, deliberately, Colin Thane etched out the substance of Professor MacMaster's report, then the interview he'd had with the hospital surgeon. Gradually, Colonel Donnan's remaining hostility thawed and gave way to reluctant interest.

'But what does it prove?' he complained. 'Maybe Herrald did lie, and maybe Kelch was as ill as you say. But how far does it take you?' A last puff at the cigarette, and he stubbed it on the desk ashtray. 'Just that Herrald may want to hide an earlier meeting because of what happened later. And you told me yourself – medically, Kelch might have been able to keep going, even with the pneumonia in full flame.'

Thane knew the argument. He'd used it against himself when he first tried to analyse the new maze of possibilities which had sprouted up before him.

'Yet here's something you told me,' he countered. 'You said General Shashkov was squeezing every drop of publicity out of the situation because it not only made us look foolish but helped build up his public image back home – that he'd been "out of favour" with some of his party pals. How much out of favour?'

'How much?' Donnan found it hard to answer straight off. 'That has to be two-thirds guesswork. It's the old, old story, pressure groups at work, charges of what they call ideological deviation, hell knows what else. If Shashkov was out of the way, well' – he shrugged – 'he wields a lot of influence. That's probably his main value to the top boys. They'd find him hard to replace.'

'And supposing this get-tough brigade decided to arrange things so that he was completely out of the way?' Thane's fingers closed hard round the pencil again. 'Where would be the best place to try it? At home, where things could be nasty if anything went wrong – or abroad, where it would be easy to shift the blame away from themselves? Wouldn't it be ideal for them to get rid of Shashkov and at the same time set him up as a martyr, use the situation to stoke up their own line, force the top boys to turn on the pressure again?'

Incredulous, Donnan started to laugh then changed his mind. He sat back, shaking his head. 'Now take it easy, Thane. This is –'

'Madness? Is it?' The pencil snapped, but Thane ignored it. 'I'm a cop – I'm supposed to deal in facts, nothing else. Right, I'll give you facts. How long is it since Shashkov's visit to Britain was announced as being scheduled? A little over three months. How long is it since Peter Herrald met Barbara Mason at a party he "just happened to go along to with a friend"? Two months. Herrald ended war service as an R.A.S.C. captain. Before that he was in the Royal Engineers. But do you know what his unit was before he was commissioned? A demolition section – explosives experts, trained for the job. I got that from Army Records twenty minutes ago.'

He saw Donnan's flickering frown and knew that, at least, had scored.

'If that's not enough, explain this away,' Thane plunged on. 'Four men were seen around the holiday chalet where Phil Moss was clubbed. Three of them left fingerprints all over the place – couldn't have cared less. But not the fourth, Colonel. A fourth man's prints were at the old cottage, on the car Serviev crashed – so what was so special about the chalet? Was it he didn't go there, that the

179

fourth man people caught a glimpse of was somebody else altogether, somebody who couldn't take chances?'

Colonel Donnan sat silent for a long moment, his mouth narrowed, a new, thoughtful look in his eyes. When he spoke, the words came slowly.

'Anything more?'

'Only little things. I've got men out, but they need time.'

Donnan nodded, his voice dulled. 'All it would need would be the right man in a high-up position over there. They know Shashkov is going to Scotland. . . . Martin Kelch is on their files and working on the trawler fleet. He has a built-in motive, friends who'd shelter him, in fact he could have been made for the purpose. Plant some other "freedom lovers" on the trawler, give them time to work on him, then make sure they get the chance to make what looks like a genuine break, and the rest follows on.'

'With Herrald already waiting ashore.' Thane slid the cigarettes across the table again. 'That import-export business could make an ideal cover for a very different type of agency.'

'And provided the orders came from the usual source, he wouldn't query them.' Donnan lit his cigarette and drew heavily. 'The contact man, the man who could have gathered all the local knowledge they would need.' A thought struck him. 'Where is he now?'

'In town. Being watched.' A grey humour wisped over Thane's lips. 'As long as Martin Kelch is unconscious and looks like dying, Herrald will sit things out. Why not? Right now everyone feels sorry for him. He's the poor devil who saw his pal killed, the man who was kept in the bottle. When the story makes the papers, he'll be a minor hero. Stolen explosives, home-made bombs – the whole thing was rigged, Donnan, all part of the play-acting with Herrald as stage manager!'

The security man cleared his throat. 'Could you use

some help?' The words meant more than they said, his complete acceptance of the turnabout.

Thane had been saving his final long-shot hunch for this moment. 'You could take Vilkas Stender off my hands, for a start.'

'You know where he is?' The little Irishman was taken completely by surprise. 'I thought he'd simply vanished . . .'

'I think I know where he'll head,' said Thane softly. 'There's one place nobody in his right mind would go searching for an Iron Curtain refugee – a ship that's ready to sail back there.' He picked up one of the scrawled notes on his desk. 'There are three due to sail from Scottish ports in the next forty-eight hours. Want the sailing times?'

Donnan's hand closed on the paper. 'As of now, this is mine. What else?'

Thane grinned at the other man's enthusiasm. 'I'll let you know,' he promised. 'It's going to be a long night.'

It was. Till three a.m., to be precise. But when Colin Thane finally surrendered to the canvas-sprung comfort of a brief sleep in the folding camp bed kept stowed in his office he knew he'd been right, knew that only one last factor was needed to complete the pattern he'd sought to reconstruct. And Phil Moss had it, was bringing it down with him when he left St. Andrews at dawn.


The big silver-grey TU104 turbo-jet carrying General Shashkov back to Moscow howled down the Prestwick Airport runway at exactly 08.00 hours on Sunday morning, a lumbering, clumsy giant which transformed into a great but graceful metal bird as it became airborne and found its own element. It gained height, vapour trailing, the sun glinting on its nose to give the watchers below a last glimpse of the red hammer-and-sickle emblem on its nose. Then, within seconds, it was a dwindling shape fading to a dot lost among the clouds.

One hour later, Colin Thane telephoned from his office in Millside to Peter Herrald's flat. When Herrald answered, Thane kept his manner apologetic while he asked the man to come over and give the signed statement he'd promised.

'Seen the Sunday papers yet?' Thane trailed all the bait necessary. 'General Shashkov's been kicking up blazes – headlines all the way. Now we've heard they've found out about Kelch. The only part of the story they don't know yet is your own – and the press brigade will probably be on to that by noon. And I've got my orders' – Thane winked across his desk at Phil Moss and Donnan – 'we've to have your statement in full before there's as much as a sniff of a reporter around. Can I send a car to collect you in half an hour?'

Herrald grumbled, then agreed and hung up.

Exactly on time, two detective constables arrived at his flat. They were polite, they were cheerful, their car was outside – and they didn't mention that since five that morning, when they took over from the previous duty team, they'd been within constant watching distance.

A few minutes before ten a.m. Peter Herrald came strolling into Thane's office. He wore a neat, tailored sports jacket and whipcord slacks and returned Thane's greeting with a lazy ease.

'How's the shoulder, Chief Inspector?'

'A little stiff, that's all.' Thane glanced at the others in the room. 'You know Inspector Moss – this is Colonel Donnan, Home Office security.'

Herrald nodded towards the little Irishman, then took the chair Phil Moss pushed forward. He was in front of the desk with Thane in his usual chair opposite. Donnan sat over by the window and Phil Moss stationed himself casually by the door, notebook in hand.

'You had a pretty rough time of it from what I've heard,' said Donnan sympathetically.

'Back here, it seems like a nightmare.' Herrald shook his

head. 'I don't know how long it takes to forget that kind of thing. Barbara said –' He broke off and glanced at Thane. 'You heard she drove me down yesterday?'

Thane nodded. 'Her mother told me. Lady Dunspar's still at the hospital.'

'I know.' Herrald pursed his lips. 'I telephoned her there this morning, just after you called. The woman's beyond reasoning with, but I felt I had to try. She said there was no change in Kelch.' He ran a hand over his thinning fair hair. 'I still feel . . . well, every now and again I get the shakes.' He fumbled in his pocket and brought out a narrow leather cigarette case. 'Mind?'

'Go ahead.' Thane pushed the ashtray towards him and struck a match for the man. Herrald cupped a steady hand over the flame, then sat back.

'Thanks. Well, do you want to get this statement over?'

'Might as well.' Casually, Thane flicked over the papers before him. 'These are my own notes of what you said yesterday. They'll save us going over too much old ground. You left Glasgow with George Shaw on the Saturday. When did you first meet Martin Kelch?'

'On the Tuesday night, outside the Tayman Hotel in Aberfeldy.' Herrald fingered the lapel of his jacket as he sat back in the chair, his eyes straying round the room. 'That was the arrangement we'd made.'

'And the first time you visited the cottage was the next day?'

Herrald nodded.

From his stance by the door, Phil Moss gave a sigh. 'Sorry, Mr Herrald – but do you mind giving answers?'

Herrald looked round, saw the notebook, and grimaced. 'For the record? All right, put down "answered yes".'

'You said things were friendly at first when you arrived up there.' Thane fiddled with the papers again. 'You had a meal with them.'

183

'Well, a pretty rough and ready one,' agreed Herrald. 'They were living on tinned stuff mostly.'

'Did you give them any food?'

'Us?' Herrald blinked. 'No. Why?'

'Just building the picture,' Thane assured him. 'You were camping, you might have had spare supplies. Now, when George Shaw found the gelignite and said he'd go for the police, you say Kelch was the one who fired the shot that killed him. I can fill in the details – but I'd like to tell you one thing.' Thane leaned forward, the smile wiped from his face, his voice ice-flecked. 'You're a liar, Mr Herrald.'

Herrald jerked in his chair. 'What do you mean?'

'A pretty good liar.' Thane strode round the desk and stood towering over the man. He reached out, took the cigarette from Herrald's fingers, and stubbed it out on the ashtray. 'But not quite good enough.'

A red flush spread over Herrald's smooth, plump face. 'Have you gone crazy, Chief Inspector? You pulled me out of that pit yourself! Colonel – look, I can't remember your name, but do you know what this is all about?'

The security chief remained impassive. 'Most of it. If it helps, I had three men at the dockside when Vilkas Stender tried to board the freighter Dubrova at Leith Docks at two o'clock this morning. Funny thing – she was due to sail with the tide at four, bound for the Baltic, first port of call Riga.' He ran one hand lightly round his collar. 'After all the trouble he went to getting off that trawler you wouldn't think he'd want to go back behind the Curtain again, would you?'

'What's Stender got to do with me?' Herrald started to rise from his chair. 'He was one of the four – that's all I know about him.'

'Is it?' Thane pushed him back down again. 'Herrald, your job was to meet up with these four and play Kelch and Lady Dunspar along as far as possible. The knight in shining armour coming to help those poor runaway sailormen. . . .' He gave a growl. 'You could have kept the fiction going until it was time to put Kelch out of the way and let your three pals get to work. All you'd have to do was tell Lady Dunspar that all four of them had rejected your help and disappeared – you could be certain she wouldn't talk, and George Shaw would probably be the same. In fact, George Shaw was a perfect alibi – because if he ever did tell what he thought was the truth, you still emerged as just a fellow who'd tried to help and been shoved aside. Only the plan went off the rails when he found out too much!'

'The whole thing's ridiculous!' Herrald saw his protest fall on deaf ears.

'Who killed Shaw?'

'I told you – Kelch.'

Thane sighed. 'There's a little point about Scottish law you maybe don't know. If a group of people join together in acts which add up to murder then the law says they're all equally guilty. And Herrald – murder by shooting, murder by use of explosives both carry a death sentence.'

'But you're wrong – completely wrong!' Herrald ran one hand over his head, his eyes bright with what could have been fear but was nearer to a fighting despair.

Thane leaned back against the desk, reached behind him for his cigarettes, and lit one, watching the man all the time. 'I'm tired, Herrald. We're all tired. So I'm going to tell you just a few of the things we've got against you. You said you didn't go to the cottage till the Wednesday. We can prove you were there on the Monday, prove it positively.'

'I – all right, that's true.' Herrald chewed his lower lip. 'But just to talk to them. That doesn't make me a murderer, does it?'

'How'd you know where to find them?'

'Kelch told me – when we spoke on the phone the second time Lady Dunspar called me.'

'She says differently. But we've traced a record of

another trunk call to your number, from a phone box less than half a mile from her home.' Thane's smile was cold. 'That was one of the things we kept working on overnight – checking telephone exchanges all along the area from where Kelch and the others first came ashore, inland to the Dunkeld area. One phone call a night, always late at night, always to your number, always a different exchange. You knew exactly how they were getting on – you had to, to play your part in the game.'

'The killing game,' grunted Donnan from his corner by the window.

Herrald sat silent now, the colour gone, his hands clenched in his lap.

'There's plenty more.' Thane's voice went on in remorseless monotone. 'A shop assistant who remembers an "uncle" buying a radio-controlled toy launch for his "nephew" – two months back, and the description is vague. But it still fits. Two months back, Herrald. Just about the time you became the sudden friend of a man who happened to work in the same hotel as Barbara Mason, then persuaded him to take you along to a party where you knew you'd meet her.'

The telephone on his desk gave a double ring and he broke off, nodding to Moss. The wiry second-in-command crossed over and answered the call, listening for a moment, thanking the voice at the other end, then hanging up.

'Kelch's condition . . .' as Herrald's head snapped up in his direction he gave a faint grin, '. . . slight improvement, Colin. Still unconscious, but he may make it now.'

'Thanks.' Thane ran a thumb along his chin and contemplated Herrald again. 'You pulled a nice double bluff with those fake raids on your office and flat after Shaw was killed. Left it to us to decide that somebody was trying to make us believe you were on the run. You scored there – but you came a cropper when it came to Martin Kelch.'

Herrald struggled to find his voice. 'Another crazy idea,

186

Chief Inspector? Kelch shot himself – everyone knows that.'

'Then maybe they're wrong.' Thane stared him down. 'You didn't know Kelch had a galloping case of pneumonia, did you? Hiding out in fields at night probably started it. Being dumped into that damp-walled stone pit fanned it on. You kept him there until you needed him, didn't you? Then gave him a clean-up and fresh clothes – but didn't you notice how weak he was? Did you think he'd just been down there too long?' The Millside chief leaned back. 'But that's only part of it – tell him, Phil.'

Moss gave an acid scowl. 'We took a paraffin test of Kelch's right hand. He'd fired a gun all right. But the doctors were already wondering about the bruise at the back of his head, a bruise which meant he could have been out cold at the time – his finger on the trigger, but someone else supplying the muscle power.' He gave a soft, comfortable belch. 'Then we found something else, when we tried to take his prints. The fingertips were raw, grazed, full of little cuts, the kind of cuts a half-delirious man might get if he was trying to claw his way out of that pit, Herrald. We tried the paraffin test again – and got sandstone particles from those cuts.'

Peter Herrald sat motionless in his chair for a moment then opened his hands and looked down at them. When he raised his head again he tried to force a smile but failed.

'You win with that one, Chief Inspector. Kelch was the man in the bottle. You've guessed the rest?'

Thane nodded. 'You raided the explosives magazine?'

'First night out. Shaw didn't know a thing until he found the stuff under the van's spare wheel just after we got to the cottage on Wednesday.' He shrugged. 'I'd been there earlier – sneaked up on the Monday while he was fishing and the others had made sure Kelch wouldn't be around. But I couldn't move the gelignite that time. Shaw had the van keys with him.'

'Who shot him?'

'Doesn't matter much now, does it?' He didn't look for an answer. 'I did. That was when we had to put Kelch on ice – he tried to make a break for it, tumbled to what was going on. We would have to have done it that night anyway. Shashkov dead and a nice, convenient suicide by a man who'd done what he wanted and was tired of running – it would have made a neat package.' He gave a slow, regretful shake of his head.

Colonel Donnan stirred by the window. 'The two other tries?'

'Just part of the build-up. I'd scheduled the job for the Old Course, and hopped down the bottle once things got under way.' Herrald gave a weak grimace. 'Well, it flopped. But you'd found me and Stender had already taken Kelch down to the harbour.' He gave a pale ghost of a smile. 'No problem. We'd "borrowed" a car. Stender's job was to get rid of Kelch half an hour after he heard the bomb go off, then get out.' The words were bold, but there was a tremor creeping into his voice and his hands were clenched tight again.

'Want to tell us more?' Donnan spoke coaxingly. 'I've got men searching your flat right now.'

'They won't find much that matters – not the kind of thing you're after.' Herrald stood up. 'Maybe later, Colonel – maybe not. I've done enough talking for a spell.'

Thane gave a faint nod. Phil Moss came forward and took a light finger-and-thumb grip on Herrald's sleeve. They went out of the room and the door closed.

Colin Thane felt suddenly tired. But one last thing remained. 'What about Stender, Colonel? When will you deliver him?'

The security chief sucked hard on his teeth, a harsh, unpleasant sound. 'I held out on you, Thane, I'm sorry, but sometimes I have to play dirty. My men saw him all right, but they were under orders to do nothing to prevent him boarding the ship. He sailed on it.'

Thane stared at him, dumbfounded.

'This is why.' Donnan pulled a long white envelope from his inside pocket. 'I told Shashkov the whole story before he left for the airport this morning. Told him if Stender was picked up when the ship docks at Riga that's his affair. Shashkov will take care of his end of the business, you've got Herrald and I've got this.' He nodded towards the envelope. 'It's a letter from Shashkov for release to the press. His thanks to the British Government for their swift action in stamping out "hired assassins from an outside agency". There won't be another propaganda cheep about the whole business.'

'A diplomatic agreement?' Thane didn't try to hide his feelings. 'What about Herrald? You can't hush up his story when he comes to court.'

'Nobody will try to.' Donnan walked towards the door then turned. There was a strange expression on his face, almost a pleading for understanding. 'But the law needs only certain evidence to find a man guilty, Thane. What doesn't affect the verdict doesn't need to be given, does it?' He went out, closing the door quietly behind him.

Chief Inspector Thane went over to the window and stood looking out at the grey tenements around. Martin Kelch should pull through now – and the elderly woman waiting at his bedside could be counted on to help him mould that new life he craved. Well, it was one dividend, perhaps the only one.

He glanced at his watch. He had time to go home for lunch, maybe even take the dog for a walk before he ate. And afterwards he could give MacLeod a hand on the scheduled raid on the pitch-and-toss school. It suddenly seemed very important, a return to ordinary things.

He took his hat from its peg and headed for the door.